PROLOGUE

WINTER'S FIRST CHILL WIND BLEW ACROSS THE PRAI-
rie, bending the long grasses that had been bleached
and dried to the color of dust. It chased a bit of paper
down the main street of the small town and set the general store sign swinging. Horses tied to hitching posts
tucked their tails against their hindquarters, lowered
their heads, and flattened their ears. A moaning sound
came through the single window of the tiny jail.

The young woman in the cell, filthy and haggard,
heard but did not listen, as she had once listened to the
wind in the treetops that were her shelter, or over the
plains that were her path. She felt dead to the world
already. Certainly the cold did not affect her. She was
used to surviving its treacheries. She was warm, in
fact, within the bearskin cape she had cured and fashioned herself.

Footsteps approaching her cell door did not arouse her interest any more than the lonely sigh of the prairie wind. Neither did the smell of beans and coffee.

"Got yer lunch, lady," the sheriff announced needlessly.

The young woman did not stir.

"Yer gunna die hungry."

"Just as long as I die, what do you care?"

The sheriff had no answer. He seldom knew what to say to the strange young woman. He cursed the fates that had delivered her to his door and the jury that had convicted her, no matter how much he had wanted it and had a hand in it. She had become famous, much more than he had known, a bloody legend in the southwest and central plains. He suspected he was going to become infamous for hanging her. He only wished he'd known a little bit more about her when he'd let her get the best of him and thrown her in the cell.

"Suit yourself," he mumbled, and returned with the tray to his cluttered desk. He thought about eating the food himself, but found he had no appetite. Just as well they were going to hang her at dusk. Then life would get back to normal.

"Good afternoon, Sheriff."

"Afternoon, Father." The sheriff glanced at the priest only briefly. He had never been a churchgoing man, and the sight of the cleric always made him feel slightly guilty. "Want me to unlock the door so you kin set inside with 'er?"

"If you please."

The sheriff sighed as he pushed his bulk out of the chair. He unlocked the cell door, but left the priest to open it himself, and returned to the desk.

"Miss Rodriguez?"

She had not meant to look up, but the sound of the long-forgotten name caught her by surprise. "You know that's not what I'm called," she said without expression.

"Louisa, then."

"That name, too, belongs to the past. It's as dead as I am. I don't need you, Father."

Her black eyes burned into him. The priest shifted uncomfortably on the stool he had placed opposite her narrow cot.

"I know something about you," he persisted. "I know you have put your life, your faith, in the hands of another. In the hands of a man. But he cannot help you now. Only God can help you."

The young woman spat defiantly. "God has never helped me, priest. He never helped anyone I loved."

"His ways are mysterious, Louisa."

"You speak the truth at last. Now you can go."

The priest ignored her. "That person you put your

3

faith in led you down the wrong road. It's time to cleanse your spirit, confess and repent, prepare yourself to tread God's pathway."

The young woman's features softened almost imperceptibly. The trace of a smile appeared at the corners of her generous, sculpted lips. "The path I chose wasn't traditional, I admit," she said agreeably. "It was surely not the life a priest would approve of. But I don't think my choice was necessarily condemned by God either. And if, as you and your kind would have us believe, God is a loving God, He would very much approve of my life. Because it was filled with love, Father. Glorious, passionate, enduring love."

The priest colored, as she no doubt meant him to.

"Oh, I know what you're thinking," the girl continued. "Our union was never sanctified by the Church. But I really don't care. I did what I did, lived as I chose. Now I'm going to pay. But it's ironic, you know. The crime I'm going to pay for I didn't even commit."

The priest cleared his throat. He did not want to debate guilt and innocence. He had never met a prisoner who admitted their guilt. "Repent then, child, for the things you did do, the sins you did commit."

The young woman remained silent and stretched out on her cot. She folded her hands on her abdomen and turned her face to the wall. The small sounds the priest made as he left the cell went unheard, as did his final muttered blessing.

Had she sinned?

Thou shalt not kill.

Yes, she had sinned.

Did she repent?

Not for a moment. Those who died had deserved to die.

Had she put her faith and trust in a man, when she should have put it in God?

Yes. Oh, yes.

A key clanged against the lock. "It's time, lady."

The first real fear assailed her, a ball of churning nausea in her gut. Her strength seemed to fail her when she tried to stand. She rose shakily to her feet, and the buffalo cape slithered from the cot to the floor. She bent to retrieve it, but the sheriff's voice halted her.

"You'll have to put yer hands behind you, lady."

Of course she would. She let her eyes linger on the cape just a moment longer, let the memory and the meaning have a last, lingering tug on her heart—then she complied and the sheriff secured the handcuffs. She shivered briefly in the cold, but knew the physical discomfort wouldn't last much longer. The shiver turned to a shudder of horror. A last glance at the buffalo hide washed away the adrenaline surge of fear.

"You walk on ahead of me. And don't try nothin' funny."

It seemed a stupid thing to say. She walked out of the jail into the failing light of dusk. The wind picked up her heavy, matted hair and lifted it briefly from her shoulders. The sheriff poked her in the middle of her back.

"Keep movin'."

The whole town had turned out, what there was of it. Men stood in the dusty street, while women and children were arrayed on the wood-planked sidewalks. They drifted along behind as she walked to the gallows.

The structure was silhouetted against the final pink light of the prairie sunset. The last sunset she would ever see. She was going to hang. Now.

Her bowels turned to water, and she was momentarily afraid she would shame herself.

Hanging. It was her only fear. Hanging. Not death.

And then she felt him, sensed his presence. Her fear floated upward from her and was blown away on the wind. She mounted the gallow steps.

He was near her. She had always known when he was near. The connection between them had been there from the first. It was strong, so strong. Someone slipped a hood over her head.

She wasn't sure how he would save her, but she knew he wouldn't let her hang. He knew her fear. They had made a pact. He wouldn't let her die by hanging. She trusted him.

The noose settled around her neck. Tightened.

At that moment she heard the thunder, the thunder of hooves. Someone screamed, a voice in the crowd.

And then there was no more time for thought.

Her mind numbed and a long-forgotten prayer tumbled from her lips. The floor fell away from beneath her feet.

In the last moments of consciousness, Blaze heard the odd thunder of hoofbeats, a solid *thump* right behind her, and then she started swinging.

A single shot rang out.

CHAPTER ONE

NOTHING WAS MORE BEAUTIFUL OR WELCOMING THAN the high desert in the spring. Louisa could feel the warmth of the sand through the thin leather of her sandals as she walked along ahead of her burro. The familiar fragrance of bushy, blossoming mesquite was a balm to her senses, and the startling green of the leafless paloverde tree was a delight to her eyes. Tall and stately saguaro cacti were comforting sentinels as she passed among them. Mountains surrounded her like a blessing. She was home, in the place of her birth, the place she loved and never wished to leave. She was happy.

And she was hungry.

The rumbling in her stomach was fierce. She felt she hadn't eaten in days, although her mother had sent her out that morning with a handful of corn tortillas. Soon, however, she would be home. The sticks she had collected would rekindle the kitchen fire, and there would be fresh tortillas, beans, and perhaps a stringy desert jackrabbit, if her father and brother had been lucky. Tomorrow, after they had cooked most of the day, there would be prickly pear jelly from the luscious, red cactus fruits she had carefully harvested. Louisa's stomach grumbled again with impatience. It covered, momentarily, the sound of approaching hoofbeats. Then the ominous, distant thunder came to her ears.

Louisa froze. The burro's ears pricked forward, and he raised his head, nostrils testing the air.

They needed somewhere to hide. At once. Riders, in these days and times, almost always boded evil. Louisa cast about her desperately.

Mesquite might hide her, but not her animal. The foothills of the bare, brown mountains shimmered tantalizingly in the heat, but were too far away to reach in time. Her only hope was an arroyo, a crack in the earth, a gully, formed by runoff rains from the mountains. But the only way to find one in the flat terrain was to stumble upon one. Louisa started to run.

The burro did not hesitate to follow. He had followed the girl every day of his life since being weaned from his dam. Never had he known an angry word, or the prod of a stick, and he trotted briskly at her heels. The bundles on his back bounced against his gray-haired hide.

Louisa's path was tortuous. Rock and boulders strewed the sand. Barrel cacti were interspersed with patches of prickly pear and the occasional, dangerous cholla, poised to break off and cling to her should the vibration of her step draw too near. Lizards skittered away in advance of her flying feet and, growing ever closer, the cloud of dust raised by many hooves.

Abruptly, the ground crumbled beneath her feet, and Louisa found herself falling. She had come too quickly upon the edge of the arroyo, and the soft, dry earth could not support her. She tumbled to the smooth, sandy bottom of the gulch. Her burro slid down the slope she had made, and stood over her, completely unperturbed. Louisa scrambled to her feet.

She heard them clearly now, the rhythmic pounding of the hooves and the chuffing of the horses' breath. She ducked instinctively, although the sides of the arroyo were higher than her head.

Who were they? Miners? Another group in the seemingly endless stream headed to California? A motley lot, they were known to take whatever they wanted or needed along their way.

Or was it a band of Apaches, traditional enemies of her people? Louisa's blood ran cold. She had once had a friend near her own age, a beautiful girl full of promise. She now slaved in an Apache camp, counted as mere chattel of the brave who had captured and,

11

hence, owned her.

Or was it someone even worse?

Louisa did not know she had begun to tremble until she felt a weakness in her knees. Her breath came in shallow, panting gasps. She sank to her knees and leaned heavily against her burro's sturdy side.

Madre de Dios, she silently prayed. *Deliver me from the devil*.

For devil, indeed, he was. A man with no soul who collected Apache scalps for their bounty. And when he could find no women, or children, or braves of the tribe he sought, he indiscriminately killed her people, took their scalps, and trimmed them to look like the ones that would fill his pockets with bloody dollars. Despite the heat, Louisa shivered uncontrollably.

Because the hoofbeats were fading away. Fading, but not toward the west and north, where she longed for them to go. They disappeared to the east, toward the small village where she lived with her parents, her baby sister, Inez, and adored older brother, Tomas.

Fear replaced the bones in her limbs with water. Her heart hammered so painfully against her ribs she thought they might break.

Calm. Be calm, she told herself. *It is only a band of my people riding on some urgent errand*.

But her people had few horses. They had fewer errands of urgency in this quiet corner of the desert.

And then she was running, running down the bed of the arroyo as fast as her legs had ever carried her. Somewhere outside the immediate focus of her mind, she heard the three-beat rhythm of her burro galloping along behind her. But her only thought was for her family. And what she might find when she reached her village.

Santa Rita crouched against the foothills like a timid fawn resting in the protective shadow of its mother. Even its color was like camouflage, tan and dusty, almost indistinguishable from the barren hills behind it. The narrow trail that led to the cluster of poor adobe huts was a considerable distance from the main road that traveled northward into Tucson and, as a result, few came upon the village purely by chance.

So why did a dust cloud hover over the town like a veil of pale gauze? Not one horse, but many, had ridden into Santa Rita.

Louisa bent over, gasping for breath. The fear that crowded her chest made it seem even harder to breathe. Sweat poured from her overheated body and fell like rain to dampen the earth. She willed her heart to slow that she might run again.

Riders had come to Santa Rita. A band of men,

riding hard. For what purpose?

An answer came immediately to her silent question, an answer that had come before and launched her headlong flight for home. For Louisa knew, with sure and certain instinct, that it was not miners or Apaches.

She could breathe again. She started to run.

The slap of her sandals on sand came but vaguely to her ears. Her body was damp with sweat, and her mouth was dry. Terror was a hand that tightened around her throat.

Because she could hear it now, the screaming. Men shouting. Gunshots.

The wall around the village was primitive; organpipe cacti planted close together. Even when they died, their skeletons left a prickly barrier. A barrier she could see through to the carnage beyond.

"*Mama . . .*" The cry flew from her throat, mindless, as she ran through the open gate. A gate she doubted had ever been closed. The Mexican-American War was over. Her people lived in peace. Even the warlike Apaches had become scarce, almost wiped out by the man who hunted their scalps. The man who now took the scalps of her people.

Louisa became an animal, stripped of all humanity. A feral growl came from deep within her breast. Her lips curled into a snarl as she bared her teeth. She hurled herself at the man nearest to her, the one who had just shot her young cousin in the back of his head.

The man's horse skittered sideways, scared by the wild thing clinging to its rider's leg. Louisa was dragged along, hands gripping the stirrup, teeth searching for flesh beneath the coarse fabric of the man's trousers. She felt blows raining on her head, and her vision clouded. She gave no thought to the fact the man had a gun and had just killed a member of her family, just as the wolf gives no thought to the hunter's rifle. She simply reacted.

And then she could see only red. Her fingers lost their grasp, and the breath was knocked from her lungs. She tasted dirt and blood. Something hit her in the ribs. A boot perhaps, or a hoof, and searing pain shot through her side. She ignored it and pulled herself along the ground, reaching blindly for something, anything.

When Louisa's hand connected with something warm and soft, her mind rebelled and kept her from the reality of what she groped. The clothing that covered it was merely a useful tool, and she used it to wipe the blood from her eyes. She pushed to her feet, turning from the corpse as she rose. It was only to see the end of life as she had known it . . . or would ever know it again.

The screams in the village had ceased, replaced by the pitiful moans of the dying. An occasional gunshot

15

ended those sounds as well. The street was littered with the dead. Rough-looking men knelt among the bodies, knives glinting in the sun until the blades were too bloody to reflect light any longer.

Louisa couldn't think why they hadn't noticed her. She couldn't think at all, in fact. Her mind was numb with horror.

They were all dead. Everyone. Women, some with children still in their arms. Old men. Old women. Everyone.

Somewhere lay her mother and her father. Little Inez. Tomas.

The air reeked of death. The sun beat down relentlessly, mercilessly. Louisa stood frozen in time and space. The world ceased to exist.

The men continued their gruesome work, stringing scalps like fish on a line. Louisa's mind still refused to function. What she looked at, what she saw, did not register. It was meaningless motion, sound, and color.

Until a shout distracted them all. Louisa's head turned with all the rest, turned to the slender youth who appeared from behind an adobe wall. Blood smeared his face and simple tunic. An old, but carefully tended rifle was raised in his arms.

Something stirred to life in Louisa's breast. The beating of her heart returned. Blood surged through her veins. His name raced to her lips, but she stifled it.

Tomas.

"Throw . . . throw down your guns," the boy ordered. His voice shook. The rifle wavered visibly in his grip. Someone laughed.

The hope that had blossomed so brilliantly dissolved into cold terror. Her brother had a single-shot rifle. All the men had repeat-shot pistols. Tomas hadn't the slightest chance of survival.

But he knew it.

"I know I'm going to die," he said in a hard voice Louisa scarcely recognized. "And I welcome it. But one of you is going with me."

"Noooo . . ." Louisa hissed, all the breath, all the life going out of her with that single word.

Another laugh, this time from a thin, weathered man, the only man still sitting on his horse. It was the cruelest sound Louisa had ever heard.

"You just made a bad mistake, boy," the man said. "You thought you were gonna die easy. I ain't fixin' to accommodate you."

It was unbelievable how cold she felt, even with the sun beating down on her head and sweat pouring from her body. Her blood was as icy as the river water in winter.

The rider nodded at a burly man bent over one of the bodies, and made a motion with his fingers. Tomas swung the rifle toward the kneeling man, and Louisa's heart rose into her throat. The big man smiled. The lightning-like scar that ran through one eyebrow and down his cheek crinkled as if with merriment.

"If you aim to shoot me, son," he said, "do it now."

Tomas's finger tightened on the trigger. Louisa could almost feel it herself. She was as taut as a bowstring. The big man rose and walked to his horse.

"Stop," Tomas commanded.

The big man kept moving. He untied the rawhide that held a lasso to his saddle.

Louisa stood transfixed, paralyzed with fear. The big man uncoiled the loop and swung it around his head.

"Best shoot now, boy," he drawled.

Tomas's eyes darted between the man with the lasso and the tall man on the horse. The rifle shook in his hands. Rivulets of water ran from his temples.

Louisa's tension was too great, and the arrow was loosed from its bow. The scream flew away from her before she could stop it.

"Tomas . . ."

Heads turned in her direction. Pistols were withdrawn from holsters. The lasso's loop floated, as if in slow motion, toward her brother.

The man on the horse grinned as he aimed his pistol at her. She knew, with absolute certainty, that he was the one who would shoot her. He was distracted for a moment, however, by the lasso's flight.

Louisa saw it settle over her brother's head and come to rest above his shoulders. She watched it draw tight. The burly man threw the end of the rope over the branch of a dead and leafless tree, even as he mounted his horse. He tied the end of the rope around his pommel, then pulled on the horse's reins.

There was not another scream in her. Horror filled every pore of her body, every drop of her blood, every centimeter of her lungs. The big man's horse began to back.

The rifle in Tomas's hands fired uselessly and fell from his grip as his fingers groped at the noose about his neck. A moment later his feet dangled above the ground. His face turned dark, and his tongue protruded. His body spasmed.

She welcomed it, the bullet. She ran to it, arms outstretched. She saw the man's face again, his grin. Then nothing. She did not even hear the shot.

CHAPTER TWO

THE MOURNFUL CALL OF THE DESERT DOVES WAS THE first thing of which she became aware. The sound was a balm to her soul, the familiar music of the morning. It heralded another day of work and love and laughter, and another day to spend amid the teeming life of the desert she loved so well. Louisa stirred, prepared to snuggle under her colorful blanket for a few more moments of the predawn hour, but the movement brought only searing pain. Her side ached so badly she could not take a deep breath, and there was something terribly amiss with her head. She tried to open her eyes, but they seemed to be glued shut. Louisa scrubbed her fists against her eyelids.

The motion intensified the pain. But she embraced it, for it covered something darker, something so horrible that nausea instantly filled her stomach.

Louisa rolled over and retched onto the dry ground. Lightning flashed in her rib cage; thunder crashed in her head. And when she opened her eyes at last, memory engulfed her.

Louisa lay very still, the mental pain as great as the physical. The torment was so overwhelming, she was afraid that if she moved she might break. She concentrated instead on her breathing. Slow breaths, not too deep, until her heart found its rhythm. Then, carefully, she got to her feet.

Down the street a buzzard flapped lazily into the air. Others circled. They warily eyed the grisly remains. Louisa forced herself to do the same.

Unless someone had miraculously escaped, she was the only one of her village left alive. Bodies sprawled everywhere. All except one, still hanging, and from that she kept her eyes averted. At least he had not been mutilated.

There were others, she noticed, that were intact as well. Not every scalp had been taken; the old ones, for instance. Why? Because their hair was gray and would bring no bounty dollars? Why kill them, then? Why take every single precious life in the village?

Something pushed at Louisa from deep inside, nudged at the dead place that had once housed her soul. It pushed so hard a feral grunt issued from her throat.

They killed everyone so there would be no

witnesses, no one to tell the tale of the dead. They had shot her as well. Louisa raised tentative fingers to the fire that had burned in her temple.

The bullet had grazed her deeply. She winced, but forced herself to follow the bullet's path. It had struck her left temple and traveled on, into her hairline. Her hair was encrusted with blood.

But she was alive.

The thing within her pushed again. Her lips parted as her breath quickened. Whatever it was was huge, and wished to be free.

She was alive, alive to honor the dead.

The thing continued to swell and grow. It pushed against the back of her throat now, stinging, making it impossible to swallow. Her eyes burned.

She was alive. A living witness. The murderers had failed. Her life was not over. It had just begun.

Tears streamed from Louisa's eyes. The thing inside of her broke free, erupting into a wrenching, heartbroken sob. Emotion threatened to overwhelm her. But it was no longer strictly the emotion of loss and grief and sorrow. And what it was, would carry her through all the days and years to come, until she had exacted her revenge, and had vengeance for the dead.

Louisa concentrated on taking deep breaths until she had her tears under control. There was not time for them now. She had too much to do.

The sun rose to noon, blazing, and began its descent. Louisa did not cease from her labors. She hungered, but had no stomach for food, not with the task she had set for herself. She had stopped once for water, pulling the bucket up from the well. It occurred to her, briefly, that it might have been poisoned. But then she remembered they had meant to leave no survivors. There would have been no reason to set a trap for anyone left alive. She smiled grimly, then drank deeply and poured the remainder over her head and shoulders. The coolness was momentarily reviving.

By nightfall she estimated the trench was large enough. She had no strength left, however. She would have to finish her task in the morning.

Louisa could not, would not, return to the space she had once called her home. Instead she curled up under the makeshift roof that provided shade for the livestock corral. Manure was pungent in her nostrils, but all the animals were gone. Driven away probably, or stolen. It hardly mattered.

Spring nights on the high desert were chilly, and Louisa had no blanket. But the sand was still warm. And the blessing of sleep claimed her the moment she closed her eyes. She did not wake until she heard the

23

flapping of great wings.

The buzzards had returned. She did not mind them. They were only doing what nature had intended.

Louisa was vaguely surprised by her lack of emotion. What once would have horrified her was now merely another fact of her existence as she moved through life. Had she changed so much? Undoubtedly. There would be other changes as well, she thought, that she would discover along her way. A way that had to continue now, toward the terrible thing she had to do, had to move through, to get to the other side and go on.

The labor was not as hideous as she feared it would be. Bodies were not only mutilated, but bloated now. It was difficult to recognize friends and neighbors by their features. And she carefully covered each one in a blanket or a shawl before she dragged them, one by one, to the grave she had dug. She took extra care with the little ones, and had to swallow a painful obstruction in her throat.

The noon sun came again, and departed. There was only one family left, four pitiful bodies.

Louisa had thought to dig a separate place of burial for them, but her strength was nearly gone. It did not matter anyway. *They are together with God*, she told herself. Armed with that small bit of comfort, she faced her final test.

Her father had been shot in the face. She knew him only by his wedding ring. It was cleverly twisted, like the binding of two cords together. Louisa's mother had been so proud to give him that ring because, she had said, it was a symbol of how he had bound her to him with his love.

Louisa had to stop for a moment. Tears coursed through the grime that caked her face. She licked her lips and tasted salt. She had to focus for a time on a cactus wren that hopped in and out of the nest she had carved from the flesh of a towering saguaro. Then Louisa covered her father tenderly with a blanket her mother had woven, and did what she had to do.

She laid her mother at his side. She had taken care not to look at her face. Senaida Rodriguez had been a strikingly beautiful woman. She put little Inez in her mother's arms.

Louisa stopped again, but not because she wished it. She seemed frozen, paralyzed, as if the act, what she had just been forced to do, had taken away the last of what was in her that had kept her going. She simply couldn't move.

The sun was barely above the horizon. Sunset was brilliant with shades of salmon and pink, and an almost impossible crimson. A coyote yipped.

Louisa blinked, feeling she had awakened from a long, dreamless sleep. But a sleep that had brought her no rest. She felt heavy, ponderous, fearful her move-ments would be awkward.

Yet the final thing had to be done.

When she moved at last, it was like moving through thick, knee-deep mud. Louisa walked slowly to the bare and leafless tree that had once stood like a venerated grandfather in the center of their village.

Of all the horrors, this was the worst. Tomas was a hero. He could have run, hidden in the mountains. But he had not. He had taken their father's rifle and chosen to make his last act an honorable one. They had murdered him ignobly.

There it was again, that peculiar swelling of emo-tion in her breast, something akin to, but not quite, elation.

"You did not have your vengeance, Tomas," Louisa whispered. "But I will have it for you."

The words strengthened her. She laid a blanket on the ground and cut the rope.

That night she did not even seek shelter. Louisa drop-ped where she stood when her stamina failed at last. She slept where she fell.

At dawn Louisa rose and collected every rock she could find. It took her most of the day to stack them over the long, sad trench. When she was finished, she stood and gazed on what she had done.

There should be a priest to say words over you, but there is not, she intoned silently. *There should have been a God to watch over you. But there was not.*

Her task was complete. As was her metamorphosis.

The sunset of the third day was as brilliant as the one before it. Louisa stared at its magical colors until the fiery orange globe slipped below the horizon. The huts surrounding her lost their substance in the half light of dusk. Saguaros and mesquite beyond the village gate dissolved into meaningless shadows.

Her clothes were stiff with blood. Louisa shrugged out of them and left them lying on the ground. Naked, she turned and walked into the mountains.

CHAPTER THREE

ALL DAY THE WIND HAD BUILT. NOW IT WAS BRUTAL and drove straight down from the cold northeast. The long, once-green valley grass flattened, and the low gray clouds scudded southwest at an ever-increasing speed.

Ring bent his head into the wind and jammed his hat down tighter. His horse shook himself, as if trying to loose the cold air's grip, and continued on, nose almost touching the grass. Ring shivered, looped his reins over the saddle horn, and crossed his arms under his heavy woolen poncho.

It didn't do him a bit of good. The icy wind cut right through and chilled him to the bone. Worse, he thought he felt a windblown snowflake sting against his cheek.

"Damn pelouses," he muttered with uncharacteristic emotion. There were few things he hated more than being cold and wet. And he had no one to blame but himself. "Damn horses. Damn *me*."

Ring glanced up from under the brim of his hat and eyed the herd of animals that straggled along in front of him, bent to the wind, tails streaming out behind them. There were bays, grays, and buckskins, a black, a couple of sorrels . . . and the dang spotted horses, the pelouses, the cause of his current misery.

"Ring. Hey, Ring." A youth with a too-big hat pulled down over his long, dark hair rode up beside his boss's bay mare and reined his own mount to a walk. "What'chou wanna do?" he shouted over the gale. "We ain't gonna get much farther in this. Gotta turn tail and tough it out if we don't find shelter soon."

Ring answered without taking his eyes from the herd. "Prescott's not too far ahead. We'll hole up there 'til this blows over."

"*If* it blows over," the youth mumbled to himself. He was hungry, shivering, and not, generally, feeling optimistic.

"Ride on back and tell Rowdy," Ring added. "Town shouldn't be more than two, three hours ahead."

The boy, Sandy, nodded and turned his horse back toward the south. Pushed now by the wind, the going wasn't as hard, and he let his mount move into an easy lope. Within moments he spotted Rowdy's cook wagon as it bumped along behind his team of patient mules.

Sandy Long was misnamed and he knew it. More importantly, he knew why. Although he stood only five foot two and sported a luxuriant crop of jet-black hair, his daddy had been Sandy Long, so now he was, too. Rowdy, however, was a different story.

Nobody had a daddy called Rowdy. And the old man certainly hadn't earned his moniker from his behavior. There never had been, Sandy thought, a more taciturn human being in the history of the race. Rowdy hardly ever opened his mouth, never got excited, and sure never seemed to have a good time. He never drank and he didn't seem to take any pleasure from food, despite the fact he earned his living as a cook. There'd never been any women Sandy knew of. So why the name Rowdy he'd never know.

"Hey, Rowdy," he shouted when he'd drawn close enough.

The old man neither blinked nor took his watery blue gaze from the trail ahead.

"Ring says we're gonna make for Prescott, quit there for awhile."

Still no response. Sandy's irritation mounted. He'd never gotten used to Rowdy's silences and guessed he never would.

"We're stuck in this weather now cuz of those damn pelouses," he complained loudly. Rowdy didn't answer, but Sandy hadn't expected him to. He just felt like grousing. "Ring just had to have 'em, but hanged if I know why. He haggled with them Nez Perce Injuns over the price 'til the weather moved in, and now we're all gonna freeze our tails off. We probably ain't even gonna make it to Westport afore hard winter sets in. And for what? Bunch of damn spotted horses?"

The mules plodded along. The wagon bounced over the uneven ground, and Rowdy remained stoically silent. Sandy grimaced. He was never going to figure Rowdy out, and was probably never going to be able to figure Ring either. He was a fair boss, a fine hand with horses, and an all around good, honest man.

But he had a strange streak. Every once in awhile he did something Sandy simply couldn't understand. Like having to have those funny-looking horses the Nez Perce were breeding. Having to have them so bad they were probably going to spend the winter in Fort Laramie instead of Westport. Hell, they'd be lucky if they even got out of Arizona at this rate.

They were already a year behind because of the detour they'd taken to Nez Perce country, then back to Phoenix, where Ring's mama was sickly. A year behind and a year's profit behind, too. They only made money when they sold their string of horses, and Ring only liked to sell them in Westport. He made good money there selling his well-trained animals to the settlers heading out west.

But it looked like they weren't even going to get *out* of the west again this year. It was only September. How could there be snow at this elevation in September?

Thoroughly disgruntled, Sandy kicked his horse into a lope. In a few minutes he had caught up with the herd, heads down, struggling along into the wind. He squinted toward the distance, trying hopefully to spot a cabin or a ranch house, something that would tell him they were getting closer to town. There was nothing ahead, however, but brown hills covered in buckskin-colored grass, and the barren, rocky mountains behind them. Scattered snowflakes blew against Sandy's face.

Sandy's shivering progressed to teeth chattering, and he hugged his arms to his chest. He had to do something, warm up, get out of the wind, anything but trudge on and slowly freeze to death.

Then Sandy spotted Ring. His head was still bent, long, sun-streaked brown hair falling over the back of his collar, arms still crossed beneath his poncho. Sandy wondered if he even felt the cold. Nothing ever seemed to bother Ring Crossman.

But it bothered Sandy Long.

Ring's mount shied a little when Sandy galloped his horse up behind him. It didn't startle Ring. His tall, supple body simply moved in perfect concert with

32

his mare, as if he had known she was going to jump to the left. Sandy grudgingly admired his boss's almost-instinctive horsemanship.

"Sorry, Ring," he apologized. "Didn't mean to spook Duchess like 'at."

Ring merely shrugged and looked Sandy's way with a small, patient smile.

"I been thinking, Ring," Sandy continued. "Maybe I should ride ahead, scout the town, you know. Make sure we're on the right track. I'd hate to miss Prescott in this." He looked up, deliberately catching a face full of snowflakes.

Ring's smile never faltered. Year after year he had ridden this trail, catching the wild ponies, or buying and trading horses from the Indians, breaking and selling them to the settlers who traveled west in an apparently ceaseless stream. He had long ago memorized even the smallest, most insignificant landmarks. Across hundreds and hundreds of miles of mountains and wilderness he had never been lost, and seriously doubted he ever would be. At any given moment in time, he knew almost exactly where he was. He knew where he was now. He also knew Sandy needed to ride.

"Go on, go ahead." Ring nodded into the distance. "When you get there, find someone who'll put on a pot of hot coffee for us."

"No problem, boss." Without further hesitation,

Sandy put his spurs to his horse's sides, leaned forward in the saddle, and headed off into the wind.

Ring chuckled as he watched the boy disappear into the horizon. Sandy was impatient, but he was a good hand. He'd make dang sure that somewhere in town there was a pot of coffee brewing just for his boss. Then maybe he'd start to thaw a bit. Beneath his poncho Ring rubbed his nearly numb hands together.

Yessir, it was going to be a mighty long, cold winter.

It wasn't a blizzard, but neither was it a light dusting. The flakes flew against Sandy's face faster and faster as he galloped into the storm. The heavy material of his trousers dampened, along with his jacket. Only his flannel shirt and long johns were still dry, but he no longer cared. Straight ahead he was finally able to see a puff of smoke that meant civilization.

Sandy's pony also seemed to sense the journey's end was near. He extended his gallop, neck stretched and ears flat to his head, mane and tail streaming banners, legs pumping rhythmically. The cowboy on his back rode lightly, completely in sync with his mount. When the valiant cow pony stumbled, therefore, his rider went down with him, gracefully, still in perfect harmony with his mount. There was a sharp crack, like a breaking stick, and a forward roll, both yet together. Then they started to tumble.

It all happened slowly in Sandy's mind. He felt his horse break his stride, knew he was going to stumble. Heard the animal's leg fracture. Experienced the forward motion of their fall. There was one primary thought in Sandy's mind as everything occurred quickly yet sluggishly.

Jack had been a good horse. He'd liked him the first time he'd ridden him. They'd been of one mind since the first. It happened that way sometimes, when the horse knew the man and the man knew the horse, right off like that. But it didn't happen often, and he was sad. He was going to miss Jack.

Then the wind was knocked out of him, and he rolled violently through the grass. He heard Jack squeal. He felt an extraordinarily sharp, bright pain in his thigh, another in his head. He saw a sunburst.

And blackness.

Ring knew something was wrong, but it didn't register right away. He was thinking about his hands, unfeeling chunks of ice, yet not too unhappy about it. They'd be warm soon. He'd hold them out over a stove, turn them one way, then the other. He'd cradle a steaming mug of coffee, too hot at first to drink, then just right. The liquid would sear a line down his gullet, into his belly, and spread out eventually through his entire body. Hell, he wasn't even upset about those spotted horses anymore. He liked them. He was glad he'd taken the time to parlay with the Nez Perce. Everything seemed all right now with warmth on its way.

Trouble was, Ring realized at last, that what he was looking at up ahead was not an unusual couple of rock formations. He kicked his mare into a slow lope and picked up the reins as she moved into her rolling gait. The herd also picked up its pace as he moved around its south side. But they soon dropped back to a trot, then a walk. Ring galloped ahead.

It was the horse, Jack, he spotted first. The animal was still trying, vainly, to get up. Ring saw why as soon as he pulled to a halt by the stricken pony.

It would have been the front leg that broke first, Ring knew, sending man and mount to the ground. Sometime during their tumble and fall, the left pastern had snapped. Jack would never get up again.

Ring drew his pistol as he dismounted. "Good old Jack," he murmured. "Good horse." He stroked the animal's long, blazed face until the horse calmed and lay still on the ground. Ring fired a single bullet into the pony's brain. He strode quickly to the fallen rider.

Sandy lay unconscious, sprawled at an unhealthy

angle. At a worse angle was the boy's thigh, bent halfway up like an extra knee. Ring knelt and felt for his pulse.

"Well, darn you, Sandy," Ring muttered. "Least-wise you're still breathing."

Ring stood up slowly and ran his thumb along the hard edge of his jaw. His mare nudged him, and he absentmindedly stroked her neck. Mind made up as to what he was going to do, he pulled his rifle from its saddle sheath and emptied it of ammunition. On the left front of his saddle he'd tied a pair of hobbles; on the right was a lariat. He unloosened it and knelt again at Sandy's side.

"Good thing you're out cold, boy."

Ring didn't even look up as the herd slowly passed, stopped, heads lowered to pull at the dry, brown winter grass. Moments later the rattle and clatter of the cook wagon ceased and Rowdy appeared at his side. The wind had let up, and the snow fell softly downward.

"Hold his shoulders," Ring ordered quietly. As Rowdy moved into his position, Ring took his place at Sandy's feet. He straightened the boy's leg, got a good grip on the broken one, and yanked.

Sandy groaned and his eyelids fluttered. "Go back to sleep, son," Ring said. "You're not going to like this next part much better." He aligned the rifle along the outside of Sandy's leg and wrapped it with the rope.

"Now what?" Rowdy asked when the leg had been secured in its makeshift splint. The brim of his battered black hat was white with snow.

"Now you help me heft him into the wagon, and then make a fire and put on a pot of coffee. I've been dreaming about hot coffee for too long now, Rowdy. It's about time I had me some."

The snow didn't last long after the wind fell. During the night, however, the temperature dropped sharply. Ring woke to a world coated in a frozen crust of white.

Rowdy, who always seemed to be up first no matter what time a man woke up, had already made a pot of coffee and was heating bacon and beans over the fire in a cast-iron skillet. His morning greeting consisted solely of casting his gaze momentarily in Ring's direction.

It was so cold Ring's buckskin leggings were stiff, and he rolled out of his blanket with reluctance. He hadn't removed his boots the night before, and all he had to do to prepare for his day was run a hand through his long, streaked hair and pull his hat down to his head. He stood up and straightened his poncho.

"I slept real soundly," he remarked, and stamped his feet to hurry their circulation. "You hear anything from Sandy?"

"He was restless," Rowdy replied without elaboration. "Here, eat before you go," he added, and shoved a plate toward Ring. "I'll wake and feed him, too."

Ring's brows arched slightly. "How'd you know I was going?"

"What choice you got?"

None. Sandy needed a proper splint and shelter. Both he and Rowdy knew that the sawbones in Prescott, assuming he still lived there, wasn't fit, or sober enough, to doctor a dog. He'd have to go back the way they'd come. And bouncing along in a cook wagon was no way to go. The pain would kill the boy. Ring turned away from the sight of Sandy's frightening pallor and faintly bluish lips.

"There's a horse doc back in Bumblebee that's as good as any in these parts."

Rowdy's response was a single, brief nod.

"Sorry, Rowdy. You wanna go on and wait for me with the horses in Prescott?"

"I'd best follow you. That boy ain't goin' anywhere this winter."

Ring sighed heavily. It was another setback he didn't need and couldn't afford. Still, as Rowdy had said, he had no choice. He saddled a horse for Sandy and tried to put the thought of the boy's pain out of his mind, for it would be almost unimaginable, he knew. Hopefully, the boy would lapse in and out, mostly out, of consciousness.

For an old man Rowdy was surprisingly strong. He helped Ring lift Sandy onto a muscular buckskin gelding, a horse Ring liked for his particularly smooth gaits. Sandy gritted his teeth, but a groan escaped him and sweat popped on his brow in spite of the cold.

"Sorry, son," Ring apologized softly. Rowdy handed him a lariat dug from the jumble of supplies in the back of the wagon. "And I'm sorry to do this, too, but you sure as hell don't want to take another fall."

Sandy held his breath as Ring looped the rope around his waist and upper body several times, and secured it tightly to the saddle. He tied a knot in the split reins and handed them to the boy.

"Hold on to 'em if you want. If you don't, don't worry. Buck's going to follow along real nice."

Sandy smiled weakly. "He's a good horse," he replied, voice cracked and strained. "Jack was a good horse, too. I'm . . . I'm sorry, boss."

"I'm sorry, too." Ring clapped Sandy lightly on his good leg. "But not about the horse. You ready?"

Sandy nodded, tight-lipped. Ring adjusted over his shoulder a powder horn and bullet sack, and Rowdy slung a double saddlebag, fully packed with food, flint, and steel, over the back of Ring's bay mare.

"Thanks, Rowdy," Ring said as he climbed into the saddle. The leather creaked. He gathered his reins. "We'll see you in a day or two."

Rowdy touched the rim of his hat in reply. Ring turned his mare and set off at once into a slow lope. The buckskin followed.

The pain was immediate and excruciating. Sandy fought it, but his body was far too weakened by shock. His hands went limp, and his head lolled. He swayed, but the rope held him firmly astride his mount.

Ring winced, and turned his gaze to the frozen horizon. It wasn't too far to Bumblebee. But it might just be too far for Sandy.

CHAPTER FOUR

Two days previously it had snowed, and the temperature dropped. The herd of mustangs had grown their winter coats, however, and did not mind the cold. Nor did they mind when, a mere twenty-four hours later, the mild fall weather returned. In fact they welcomed the runoff from the melted snow to the north, and galloped down the riverbed to drink their fill. Only the stallion, a rangy chestnut, held back to keep watch over his harem. When one of his mares got too close to a now-leafless cottonwood tree, he took off toward her at a gallop.

Ears flattened and teeth bared, the stallion charged the mare. Her head came up sharply, and she wheeled with a snort. She avoided the stallion's teeth by mere inches, and took off at a gallop down the riverbed.

Startled, the rest of the small band of mares also

took flight. The entire herd galloped south, splashing through the streams of runoff. The stallion brought up the rear and bucked occasionally with the joy of the run.

Soon, however, his cautious nature overrode his playfulness, and the chestnut horse slowed to a trot. This far down the river, the summer floods had cut deeply into the earth. The walls of the riverbed rose ever more steeply. The stallion did not like the feeling of vulnerability; neither the sensation of being closed in, nor the fear of a predator leaping on them from a high place. Too often in the past month some wild thing dropped from trees onto one of his band.

The mares eased their pace as well. Two or three bent their heads once more to drink from the small, diverging streams of water. Then there was a scream.

The bay mare's head jerked up, and she bucked with another squeal of terror. But she was unable to dislodge the thing on her back. She took off at a run, the rest of the herd at her heels.

An icy hand had clamped around Ring's heart. He glanced back at Sandy one more time.

The boy was unconscious again. His flesh was as white as yesterday's snowfall. The last time Ring had stopped to check on him, he'd felt Sandy's pulse and it was erratic. He feared the worst.

Bumblebee was still a couple of hours away. He was pretty certain Sandy wouldn't last that long. He could pick up the pace, sure, but that would just kill the boy quicker.

Ring considered stopping and trying to do something himself. But he didn't know what. Doctoring wasn't his strong suit. He scrubbed a fist along the edge of his jaw.

There was only one thing to do, he decided at last. Keep on moving. Like Rowdy had said, what choice did he have? Keep on moving. And pray.

Ring resisted the urge to look back at Sandy again. It would just make him feel bad, and he was already doing everything he could. He looked ahead instead, at the riverbed they approached, the path of the Agua Fria. It was generally dry in winter and only ran in summer following summer storms to the north. It was a good thing, because the Agua Fria ran straight into Bumblebee, and it would be an easier, faster ride for Sandy. The only trouble was, the banks were too steep. They'd have to ride farther along until he found a place where the bed was more shallow. It was less than a mile, Ring figured.

The landscape, what there was of it, was colored a wintry, dry brown. At this elevation there wasn't much cactus, just sage and mesquite, sand and rock. An occasional hawk soared overhead, keen eyes searching out snakes, lizards, or jackrabbits, none of which Ring had been able to spy. He found himself so lulled by the monotony of the ride he came upon the river, where it ran level with the ground, unaware. Surprised, he reined in his mare. And became aware of the thunder of hooves.

Ring was instantly and fully alert. This was not a populated area, and he was far from the main road. So he was about to confront either a band of outlaws, or a herd of mustangs. He sincerely hoped it was just the horses.

Even Sandy roused a little as the pounding of hoofbeats drew nearer. Ring sat straighter in the saddle.

They were mustangs. They ran lightly, riderless. And they weren't shod. The animals were his livelihood, and he knew them as well, he guessed, as he knew himself.

An instant later, the herd turned a bend in the riverbed and galloped into view. The sight of them quickened the pace of Ring's pulse. They were good-looking horses, in fine condition. Under any other circumstances . . .

"Dam*n*ation," Ring mumbled unconsciously. His jaw dropped.

It looked like a wild animal at first, a cougar maybe,

clinging to the bay's back. But cougars were farther up the mountains. A bobcat or a lynx? Too big. And no cat he knew of had a long, black mane like that.

Ring whistled under his breath. Then the herd spied him and veered sharply to the left. The creature on the bay mare's back had not anticipated the move. Unprepared, it sailed straight on while the mare wheeled to the east. The body landed in the riverbed with a thump and a grunt. The horses galloped rapidly out of sight.

Nothing could have amazed Ring more. Sandy momentarily forgotten, Ring swung out of his saddle and strode quickly to the girl sprawled in the river's sandy bed.

"Uh . . . are you all right?"

No response. Ring felt a prick of apprehension. She lay facedown, arms akimbo. Could her neck be broken? Cautiously, Ring knelt at the girl's side and grasped her wrist.

The pulse was strong. Most likely, she was simply stunned. Ring took a deep breath, got a careful grip, and eased the girl over onto her back. His heart did a funny little jump in his chest.

Ring didn't have much time to contemplate the girl's extraordinary beauty. Her eyelids fluttered open. And her eyes went wide with terror.

"Whoa, there. Easy," Ring soothed, as he had a

thousand times before with skittish horses. And as with skittish horses, it didn't always work.

The girl scrambled to her feet, prepared to bolt. Her eyes darted about as she backed slowly away from Ring, like a cornered animal assessing its chances to escape.

"Hold on now," Ring said. "I ain't fixin' to hurt you. Anyway, looks like you already did a pretty good job of that yourself."

Though blood ran down her shins from skinned knees, the girl did not acknowledge Ring's comment in any way. But she did stop moving.

"Look if you're . . . if you're okay, I'll be moving on. I got me a real bad hurt boy over there, and I need to get him into town."

It was Ring's turn to back away. The girl watched him for a moment, then her gaze slid in Sandy's direction. Her expression of terror softened.

Hope leaped suddenly in Ring's breast. "You . . . you wouldn't know anything about doctoring, would you?"

The girl's features hardened in a way that vaguely frightened Ring. "I only know about burying," she said.

The flat tone of her voice increased Ring's curious sense of apprehension. He tipped his hat to her and took another step backward. His fear for Sandy had returned in spades. He didn't even stop to question what such a lovely young woman was doing all alone in the middle of nowhere riding a wild mustang bareback. Something about her seemed to suggest she would have a very good answer. And he wouldn't like what he heard.

"I'll be getting on, then. Good day to you."

He felt the girl's eyes burning into his back when he turned around. He fitted his left foot into the stirrup.

"Wait."

He froze at her terse command.

"That boy's dying."

"I guess I know that, ma'am." He swung into the saddle.

"Follow me."

Ring hesitated only a moment. The girl was strange. The whole incident was strange. But she was right. Sandy was dying. He might as well stop here. It was as good a place as any to die.

The girl took off at a run. He was surprised by how quick she was. He reined his mare around and followed.

CHAPTER FIVE

LOUISA'S KNEES ACHED A LITTLE AS SHE RAN. THEY had taken the brunt of her fall from the mustang. But she ignored the pain. It was nothing. She had buried her entire village with at least one broken rib, if not more. She was certain the knotty lump under her left breast would remain with her for the rest of her life. She had other reasons to run lightly, swiftly, over the uneven ground.

In almost two months, Louisa had seen no one. She had wished it that way. It was that very reason she had made her home amid the cottonwoods at the river's bend. No one came this way. No one. Until now.

Louisa did not turn to see if they followed. She knew they did. She could feel the vibration from their horses' hooves close behind. She felt something else as well.

There was no harm in the cowboy or his young friend. As soon as she recovered from the shock of her fall, and finding herself almost literally in a stranger's arms, she had known she had nothing to fear. Goodness almost seemed to emanate from the man. And she felt genuine distress for the injured boy. He was barely older than Tomas.

So she had volunteered to help. Although her offer was not entirely altruistic.

A tiny spark of hopeful excitement warmed Louisa's breast. The hand of fate, perhaps, had guided the cowboy, and his horse, to the cottonwoods at the river's bend.

The high country, several days north of where she had once lived, boasted only a few prickly pear cacti among the rocks and ubiquitous mesquite. Louisa easily dodged the minor obstacles in her path and soon had the leafless grove in sight. She wove her way through the trees to the eccentric dwelling she had fashioned for herself, and disappeared inside. She heard the horses come to a halt.

Ring had never seen anything like it. He never would have been able to imagine anything like it either. The main part of the dwelling, it appeared, was an abandoned shepherd's hut. Around it the girl had built a makeshift fence of fallen limbs and branches, lashed together with long, fine twigs, probably water-soaked to make them pliant. She had placed other limbs crosswise over the top of the rude structure to make a kind of shelter that surrounded three-quarters of the hut. Ring shook his head in wonder.

"Take the boy off the horse," came a voice from within the shadows. "Lay him by the fire."

Ring dismounted and went quickly to Sandy's side, anxiety once again tying a knot in his stomach. As gently as possible, he untied the boy's necessary bonds and took him in his arms. His weight seemed nothing, and Sandy didn't so much as moan when his bad leg slid down over the saddle leather. Ring felt sick.

"Here," the girl directed. "Bring him over here."

Ring entered the shade of the peculiar shelter and saw through the open door of the hut that she had made a deep, soft bed on the floor with blankets and furs. Ring lifted his brows, and when she nodded he knelt and laid Sandy down. The girl took over at once, carefully bundling the boy to the chin.

"Look to the fire, please," she asked him. "You'll find a pot full of water. I'll need it boiling."

Ring hesitated before he moved to do her bidding. Sandy was as still as death. But he lived, for the girl took a dipper of water from a bucket and held it to his lips. When he didn't react, she parted them gently with her fingers and tried again. Though a good deal spilled over his chin, he obviously took the rest. Ring saw the boy's Adam's apple bob as he swallowed.

"Please . . . the fire," the girl repeated.

Ring unfolded his lanky frame and moved to the front of the lean-to. There was a small, circular fire pit and what looked to be a pile of dead ashes. He looked about for something to stir them with, and noted a number of things. Slightly taken aback, he reached for something that looked like it might be a fire poker, and stirred the ashes.

They had been expertly banked. When he realized they were alive, he reached for a small pile of kindling that had been neatly stacked nearby and fed the warming glow. It ignited instantly. He was not surprised to find a half-full pot of water conveniently at hand, along with an obviously homemade tripod. He arranged the whole of it over the stirring blaze.

"Have you got it going?"

He supposed he had. "Yes, ma'am."

Silence ensued. Balanced on his haunches, Ring turned and peered into the hut.

The girl still patiently coaxed water down Sandy's throat. She looked up at him briefly, and Ring had the oddest sensation. For a moment it was as if he looked into the bottom of a deep, deep well. He felt dizzy, and strangely disoriented, almost as if he were falling forward, down into the depths, to a place he would never be able to come out of again. Ring shook his head and returned to his senses. The girl had resumed her task. Ring wondered if it was his imagination, or if he had really seen Sandy's eyelids flicker.

"Is the water boiling?" the girl inquired.

Ring looked into the pot. "Yes, ma'am. It is."

The girl set her water vessel by Sandy's head and rose as gracefully as a cat. She passed by him as she left the shade of the lean-to and disappeared around the corner. Curious, Ring followed.

She walked quickly through the trees to the edge of the river, knelt, and brushed dirt away from something. Ring peered over her shoulder.

A rough-hewn wooden lid was revealed. The girl lifted it, and Ring saw a hole cleverly lined with river stones. Inside was the skinned carcass of a rabbit. Ring blinked.

"I was going to roast this," the girl said. "But I'll boil it instead. The broth will be good for the boy."

Ring could only nod. He was thoroughly astonished. She seemed to read his thoughts.

"It stays cooler down there. The ground is damp." The girl returned to the shelter and disappeared inside.

Louisa was concerned for the boy's leg. Once she had him warmed and hydrated again, she had examined the broken limb. She admired the way the cowboy must have set and held it straight, but the ride hadn't done it any good. It was more swollen than it should be and probably needed to be broken and reset. But she feared that skill was beyond her. She also feared the pain would push the boy over the edge. He was barely holding on as it was. The rabbit broth, seasoned with sage and salt, would do him good.

"It's ready," Louisa said to the cowboy. "If you'd open that box over there, you'll find everything we need."

Ring did as he was asked and was surprised yet again. The wooden chest contained a cast-iron skillet, coffeepot, tin plates and cups, utensils, and small stores of coffee, sugar, flour, and salt. He took out what he thought they'd need.

"Here you go," he said, and handed the items to the girl. "It's a real nice setup you have here. Out here in the middle of nowhere like you are, mind if I ask how you manage to set such a fine table?"

Louisa looked at the cowboy and smiled slowly. She liked him. She supposed she'd tell him the truth. "I killed a man," she replied simply.

Ring swallowed. "You killed a man," he repeated stupidly.

"Yes. For the money." Unconcerned, she ladled broth into a tin cup and carried it to the boy. She touched his cheek, and his eyes opened slowly. Supporting his neck, she gently lifted his head. "I want you to try to eat a little of this. You need to get your strength back."

Ring wasn't sure he heard right. The girl before him, the girl who so tenderly nursed Sandy, couldn't possibly have just said she killed a man for money. Unnerved, he said the first thing that came to his mind.

"Well, he must've needed killing, then."

Louisa allowed herself the luxury of another small smile. It had been a long time since any humor had entered her heart.

"Yes," she replied matter-of-factly. "He did."

Ring licked his dry lips. It was almost too much like a very bad dream. He'd hit his head maybe, instead of the girl, and had conjured this strange place and its even stranger inhabitant.

The boy was taking the broth. Louisa even thought she saw a tinge of color in his cheeks. It would be good, she thought, good to save him. She looked up at the cowboy.

"Your friend is probably going to have a limp, but at least he'll be walking. Does he have a name?"

"Sandy," Ring said. All of a sudden it seemed a little easier to breathe. "And I'm real grateful to you."

This time Louisa smiled with genuine pleasure. "I'm glad I was able to help. And . . . the man I killed? The money was bounty money."

"Bounty money." Ring didn't think he'd ever repeated himself so much in his entire life. What was it about this girl?

"You were right. The man needed killing," Louisa continued. "Although I hadn't really meant to kill him." And she hadn't meant to tell this cowboy so much, but talking to him felt good. She hadn't talked to anyone in a long time. "He was wanted by the Mayer sheriff, dead or alive, for raping a widow lady who lived outside of town."

Ring watched the girl's face change as she related the story. Her soft and lovely features appeared to harden before his very eyes.

"He hurt her, and left her for dead. She told me he'd bragged to her that she wasn't the first, that he had a lot of notches on his gun." A short, bitter bark erupted from Louisa's throat. "So, I went after him. He wasn't hard to find. I just let myself be seen around the area, and it wasn't long before he came after me. That was his first mistake."

"And his second?"

"He didn't believe I'd shoot him if he didn't take his hands off me."

It was Ring's turn to smile. "I hope the bounty

money was good."

"It wasn't much. Mayer's a small town."

Ring nodded. "I know of it. Behind Copper Mountain to the west."

Louisa nodded. "But it was enough money to buy some of the things I needed."

The girl's expression had softened once again. A hundred questions crowded Ring's head. How had she come to be here, off by herself this way? And how had she come to earning bounty money for a living? But all that seemed a little too much at the moment. Ring cleared his throat.

"I'd just like to say again, ma'am, that I'm real grateful you were here, and we found you. I don't think Sandy would have made it, otherwise. And if you don't mind, I'd like to know your name."

There it was again, that hardening. Her eyes narrowed, too. Ring wondered what could be so difficult about such an easy question.

"I don't have a name," Louisa said in a flat tone. "Why don't you tell me yours instead?"

"Ring." He tipped his hat. "Ring Crossman, ma'am. But I guess I need to call you something. It wouldn't be proper-like, to say 'hey, you', now would it?"

To his chagrin, her expression didn't alter. "I'm sorry," he apologized quickly. "I didn't mean to offend you."

He was nice. Very nice. She hadn't meant to be so rude. "I have no name because it, along with the rest of my life, is in the past. I cannot, will not, ever go back. To any part of it. I will only go forward and do what has to be done."

He heard the apology in her tone. And had one more brief, dizzying glimpse into the deep, black well. He didn't want to look again, and understood there could be something so painful, so terrible, that she didn't want to either.

"I'm a fair hand at names," Ring said at length. "I train wild horses to sell . . . when I'm not off lookin' for a doctor, that is . . . and I have to call every one of them somethin'. I like to give 'em names after their personality, or appearance. You mind if I give you a handle I can hold?"

In spite of herself, Louisa was intrigued. Having been alone so long, she hadn't thought about a name. She supposed it was time. Besides, she was curious about what he'd say.

"All . . . all right," she said tentatively.

"Well, I don't know much about your personality, having just made the pleasure of your acquaintance. But you sure do have one outstanding physical characteristic."

"I do?" Louisa's eyebrows arched. Her hands went to her face, touching it, as if trying to find something new and different.

"Not your face," Ring said, a smile lifting one corner of his mouth. "Your hair. Here." He touched his left temple.

"There's . . . there's something in my hair?" Louisa mirrored Ring's motion.

"You mean you don't . . . you don't know?" Ring wondered how long it had been since the girl had looked in a mirror. But it was no problem. He had what she needed.

Louisa watched the tall, lean cowboy stand and go to the pack on the back of his saddle. He pulled something out, a razor it looked like, and a sliver of mirror. He handed it to her.

At first all she saw was her nose and eyes. She held the mirror farther away from her face. Her breath caught in her throat.

"It's like a blaze of lightning," she heard Ring say distantly. She touched the jagged streak that ran above her left temple and disappeared into her thick, black hair. It traced, precisely, the bullet's path.

It was also the exact replica of the scar her brother's killer wore on his cheek. The hand of God?

Or the devil?

It didn't matter. It simply didn't matter. She touched her fingers to the ragged streak of white in her hair.

"Blaze," she heard Ring say from the end of a long, dark tunnel. "How 'bout I call you Blaze?"

"Blaze," Louisa whispered. "Blaze . . ."

CHAPTER SIX

IT WAS COLD, SO COLD. BLAZE LAY WRAPPED IN HER blankets, with two of her coyote skins pulled over that, and still shivered in the predawn chill. She was sure there was frost on her nose, and ducked under the covers.

She thought she had planned so well, thought of every little thing she might need. But she hadn't counted on the cold. Never had it been this bitter in her home to the south. She had miscalculated badly. The heavy men's trousers she had purchased, and the flannel shirts, were simply not enough. Not even when she wore all three shirts at once.

The sun would soon bring its warmth, however. In the meantime, she would cower beneath the blankets. She didn't even move when she heard Ring stir and crawl out of his bedroll. She listened to the small sounds he made as he stirred the fire, then set coffee on to boil. She drowsed, inhaling the familiar and comforting aroma, and thought how nice it was to have Ring and Sandy. For this little while at least.

When she smelled bacon frying, Blaze could stand it no longer. She pulled the blanket down an inch and saw Ring hunkered by the fire. He smiled at her, and she pulled the blanket back up over her eyes.

That was the one thing that was disconcerting about Ring's presence. His . . . maleness. Under the blankets, Blaze squirmed.

He was a good-looking man, she had to admit. And she liked the way his body looked in those tight buckskins and clinging chaps. He had a kind way about him, and was wonderfully patient teaching her to ride. She liked talking to him, too. The trouble was, she feared he liked her a great deal better, and in a different way, than she liked him.

Blaze waited until she heard Ring take coffee to Sandy, and sat up. She ran her fingers through the tangled mass of her hair. Her fingers paused behind her left temple.

The white streak, jagged lightning. Her name. Her obsession. Her mission.

Suddenly restless, Blaze rolled from beneath her blankets. She stepped outside the shelter to a bucket of water she kept for washing and dipped her hands, only to find a solid crust of ice. She heard a chuckle.

"Tired of the cold yet?"

Blaze ignored him. She knew exactly where the discussion was headed. Instead, she picked up the bucket and set it next to the fire.

"How's Sandy?" she asked Ring, as if he hadn't spoken.

"Better," he replied affably. "Better every day."

"Hey, I kin speak for myself, y'know."

Smiling, Blaze approached the shed where Sandy was ensconced, and planted her hands on her hips. "You can, can you?"

He smiled back, and a blush rose to his pale cheeks. "Yes, ma'am," he said shyly.

"Then tell me how you feel."

"Like Ring said, better every day," Sandy said as his blush receded. "I'm real grateful to you, ma'am, for taking care of me."

"And I appreciate you resplinting the leg," Ring added. "My rifle sure is a lot handier to use now."

She laughed; she couldn't help it. The sound was foreign to her ears.

"Can I fix you a plate of breakfast?"

That was something else that was foreign, a man waiting on her. So many new things all at once. It was Blaze's turn to blush with embarrassment. "Thank you," she said softly, and turned away to sit by the fire.

When he had eaten, Ring tended the horses. Blaze

watched him closely. "Are you going to saddle them?" she asked at length.

"Are you ready for another lesson?"

Blaze started to reply, then realized he was teasing her. All she wanted to do was ride, and he knew that. She gave him a wry smile.

"Let's get started, then."

Blaze started for the buckskin, the horse she had ridden up to now, but noticed Ring's saddle was on him instead. She raised her eyebrows.

"You've been a good student, learned real fast. It's time you rode Duchess."

Ring's horse. She was special, Blaze knew. Did it mean she was truly learning to ride? She hoped so. The first part of her plan had been successful. She had traded her father's rifle and some cash for a holster and two pistols, and had taught herself to draw and shoot. She had been trying to learn how to stay on a wild horse's back and next, hopefully, catch one of them. Then Ring and Sandy had come along. If she still believed in prayers, she might have thought they were the answer to one.

"Are . . . are you sure, Ring?"

"I know a little somethin' about horses. And riders. Tell you what, you ride Buck this morning an' if you do as well as I figure you will, you can ride Duchess this afternoon."

Blaze was amazed by how much she'd been smiling lately. It felt good.

By noon the sun had stolen some of the chill from the air. Blaze shed one of her flannel shirts, and the three of them dined on the remains of breakfast while the horses rested. As soon as she had rinsed the dishes, Blaze was ready to ride again.

"If the horses aren't too tired, I mean."

"You're sure a determined little thing, aren't you?"

Blaze had felt lighthearted all morning. Now she felt the sudden, weighty truth of Ring's words. *Yes. I am determined. And I will succeed.*

"I can wait, if the horses need more time to rest."

Ring recognized the look in her eye. He had seen it more than once in the last several days. He felt her spirit withdraw from him as well. The inner Blaze went somewhere no one else was allowed, a place she went alone to deal with whatever it was that had followed her from the past. He rubbed his jaw.

"I have an idea," Ring said at last. "Why don't we just take a nice, quiet ride? I think the both of us could use a break, along with the horses."

Was he implying she wasn't strong enough, or fit enough, or couldn't ride Duchess after all?

As soon as she had the thought, Blaze rejected it. She felt mean even to have considered it. Over the days they had spent together, Ring had recognized her mettle and had complimented her on it.

"I'd . . . like that," Blaze replied in a subdued voice.

"Good," Ring said. He meant it. "Let's mount up. You take Duchess."

Blaze grinned and climbed into the saddle without further hesitation. She felt the difference between the two horses the moment she was in the saddle. Buck was a good, solid mount, slow and easy, reliable. Duchess was going to be quicker, more responsive. She felt the horse beneath her tense, ready for the slightest command, or movement of her body. She stroked the horse's neck and murmured soothing words.

"That was exactly the right thing to do with her," Ring said. "You have what it takes to be an outstanding horsewoman. I find it hard to believe you didn't have experience with animals before this."

"Not much to speak of," Blaze said evasively. "And I truly never rode a horse before."

"Well, you sure can ride one now." Without another word, Ring turned the buckskin away from the shelter and set off at a jog.

From the time she was a little girl, Blaze had wanted to learn to ride. She had always loved horses. She had thought the most special thing in the world would be to ride one. As soon as she had mounted Buck for the first time, she knew she had been right all along. Riding a horse was as wonderful as she had imagined it to be. Riding Duchess, however, was magical.

Merely the tension of Blaze's upper thighs as she prepared to kick the mare set Duchess off at a smart trot. They moved quickly ahead of Ring and the buck-skin. Her immediate reaction was to pull on the reins to slow the horse down, but she sensed the mare would respond to the slightest movement. Blaze tried simply leaning her weight back in the saddle, and Duchess slowed to a jog that kept perfect pace with Buck.

"Well done," Ring commented. "I thought I was going to have to teach you to ride a horse like Duchess, but you seem to have all the right instincts."

Blaze felt a flush of pleasure. "Thank you. And thank you for letting me ride her."

They were silent for a time and rode slowly to the east. They crossed the riverbed, dry now, and passed beneath two lonely cottonwoods that stood sentry on the other side. Ahead stretched rolling, tan hills studded with rocks and a few sparse bushes. The crisp air smelled dry and dusty. The sun felt good on their backs. The sky was faultlessly blue.

After a time, Ring kicked Buck into a slow lope. Using her newfound skills, Blaze simply leaned forward slightly in the saddle. The mare responded as she thought she would and moved into a lope.

Ring admired Blaze as she rode along beside him. She was a natural in the saddle. She was also one of the most beautiful women he had ever laid eyes on, though not in the traditional sense. She was petite, with a tiny waist and small, high breasts. Her shoulders were narrow and belied the strength in her back and arms. She was probably, he thought, stronger than Sandy. The black mass of her hair, highlighted by the stunning streak of white, fell past her waist, and seemed to float behind her in the wind as they rode. Her eyes were large and dark, set wide apart, and her nose was small and straight. But her most remarkable feature was her mouth, lips full and vaguely pouting, astonishingly sensuous. Unconsciously, Ring licked his lips.

Totally in tune with her mount, Blaze was unaware of Ring's regard. She was happy and totally at ease. If only she could ride forever, she thought, she would.

But all too soon, it seemed, Ring reined Buck to a walk. Their shadows were long, the rapidly sinking sun shed little warmth, and Blaze shivered. Ring didn't miss it.

"You really should think about getting a coat," he said lightly. "Or spending the winter a little farther to the south."

"Ring . . ."

"I'm serious, Blaze." And he was. The lilt was gone from his tone. "You don't realize how hard the winters can be at this elevation."

Blaze shook her head obstinately. "I'm not going back. Only forward."

"Going south isn't 'going back', Blaze," Ring said gently.

Blaze stared straight ahead, silent.

"It's only a few hours' ride to Phoenix," he persisted. "And a few hours back in the spring, back where you started from. What difference does it make? You can't go any farther north now anyway. There's snow in the mountains. And you're on foot."

Blaze looked at him sharply. He had counted on it.

"Don't think I'm going to give you, or sell you, one of these horses, because I'm not. I need them both, 'specially the shape Sandy's in." Blaze looked away, but Ring continued. "I have a herd waiting in Phoenix with my other hand, I've told you that. I'm gonna train 'em up during the winter. And I've got some nice ones. The pelouses, for instance."

Blaze's curiosity was piqued; she couldn't help it. She gave Ring a sidelong glance. "What's a . . . pelouse?"

"Spotted horses, black on white mainly. They're beautiful, really somethin' t'see. They've got stamina, and real fine trail sense. I'd be pleased to give you one,

Blaze, trained just for you. As thanks, kind of, for all you've done for us."

Blaze tried not to look at him, tried not to reveal her interest. But it was hard. She concentrated on twining her fingers in the bay mare's mane.

"Where do you . . . where do you stay when you're in Phoenix?" she inquired at length.

Ring attempted to keep the excitement from his voice. "There's a boardinghouse where Rowdy, Sandy, and I stay. But my mother has a little place, you'd like it. And she'd be proud to have you."

By way of response, Blaze glanced at the sky. It was gloriously pink. "We'd best be getting back," she said. "Sandy'll be worried. And hungry."

Ring watched her turn the mare and ride back to the west without another word. He sighed deeply. And, as he had done since the first time he saw her, put his heels to his horse and followed.

CHAPTER SEVEN

SNOW HAD DRIVEN THEM OUT FINALLY, AT LEAST A
week before Blaze thought Sandy should be able to
ride. But they had no choice. They weren't equipped
for heavy snow. Ring's supplies were with Rowdy, and
she herself, she had to admit, was simply totally unprepared. At least that's what she told herself.

The truth was, she thought as she rode double behind Sandy, hands lightly on his slender waist, the idea
of her very own horse, trained by a man like Ring, was
completely irresistible. It wasn't a setback, she rea-
soned, but a step forward, in fact. She had her pistols,
and she knew how to use them. Soon she would have
her horse, her very own horse. Then there would be no
stopping her. She looked over at Ring.

He had to resist the urge to look back at her. He
could scarcely believe his good fortune. She had not

agreed to come along until the very last moment, when he and Sandy had actually started to ride away. He had to hand it to her, she was stubborn. And skillful, talented. Beautiful. Ring rubbed a hand along his jaw and sighed.

He had convinced her to come along for her sake, yes. Certainly. But for his?

Ring laughed bitterly to himself. Throughout his adult life, women had seemed to gravitate toward him. He had never even had to pursue them. They were just there when he needed one, handy, willing. Now?

It served him right, he guessed. He should have paid more attention when he had the chance. Now he had no choice.

The land sloped ever downward. Rocky cliffs rose on either side of their trail. A dusty haze followed their horses' footsteps.

They stopped once. Blaze was concerned about Sandy. She bathed his face and made him drink most of their water. Then they moved on.

Until, at last, saguaros appeared. They had reached the valley floor, the low desert. Sand crunched beneath the horses' hooves. Mountains rose on all sides. The air was cool, but not unpleasantly so. And there was no snow.

Blaze had passed this way earlier, in the spring. She had skirted Phoenix, avoided it. She hadn't been ready. But she felt an undeniable sort of excitement at the moment.

Her village had been small, inconsequential. But all her people had not been as provincial as she and her family. A few had traveled to Phoenix. They had returned with tales of amazement, stories of the city's size and its quantity and availability of items for sale; foods, fabrics, weapons, livestock, and more. Structures never seen before. Schools and churches.

Blaze could scarcely imagine it. The town of Mayer had been wonder enough. How could anything be more grand? She was soon to find out.

It came into sight slowly at first, gently. A few buildings on the immediate horizon. But as they drew closer, the scene expanded, stretched away into the distance. Dusty streets lined with buildings packed close together, side by side, one after another, and another. And there were streets behind the main street, intersections. Wagons, of all kinds and varieties, passed on the streets. There were mounted men as well, and horses tied to hitching posts. Women, in clothes the likes of which Blaze had never seen before, strolled the wooden sidewalks.

The first large building they passed was the livery stable. Next to the stable was a large corral, and it was literally filled with fine-looking animals. The longing on her face must have been evident.

"They're mine," Ring said. "You see the spotted horses? One of them's going to be yours."

She had never thought to feel joy again. Or to be unable to resist a broad grin of pleasure.

"Could we . . . could we, please, stop and see them now, Ring?"

"Yeah, Ring," Sandy chimed. "Let's take a look at the horses."

Ring chuckled. "I wish we could. But at least I know Rowdy got them here safely. We'll come back after we've checked in with Rowdy and my mother. Okay with you?"

She guessed it had to be. Blaze nodded. And then was overcome with apprehension. Ring's mother. What would a sophisticated woman who lived in a city like this think of her? Blaze nervously ran her fingers through her hair, and glanced down at her baggy, dusty men's clothing.

"You look fine," Ring said. "Besides, my mother's not like that."

It didn't help much, but she appreciated the kindness.

"Tell you what," Ring continued. "We'll stop by the boardinghouse first and see Rowdy. You can freshen up there if you want."

"Thank you, Ring."

Blaze glanced around her with increasing wonder as

they rode down the street. She saw a general store; a post office; a place that sold ladies' apparel, including hats; saloons; and a restaurant. She looked over at Ring.

"Ring . . . what's a . . . a 'restaurant'?"

He smiled at her gently. "It's a place where people go to eat."

Blaze's brow wrinkled. "You mean, a place where people can cook their meals?"

Ring resisted the urge to chuckle. "No. It's a place where someone actually cooks for you. You pay them, and they feed you."

Blaze pondered a moment, then: "Are there many people in a place like this who don't know how to cook for themselves?"

This time Ring allowed himself to laugh. "Yes, I'm afraid so. But there are also folks who are too busy, or don't have the equipment."

"People who are too busy to cook," Blaze repeated, as if to herself.

They continued along the street to a two-story wood building with a porch on the first floor, and a balcony on the second. Blaze looked up in awe.

"This is the boardin'house, if you'd like to come in," Ring said. He dismounted and helped Sandy to do the same.

Blaze found herself torn between being too intimidated to enter such a grand structure, and wanting to look presentable for Ring's mother. She chose, finally, to try to improve her appearance.

Like the gentleman he was, Ring held the door for her, but Blaze stopped.

"Thank you, but you . . . you and Sandy go in first."

Ring understood. He let Sandy pass him and followed. Blaze entered last, timidly. When she entered the lobby, she caught her breath.

The furniture was the first thing she noticed. Never had she dreamed there could be anything like it. In a corner by the window, two deeply cushioned, maroon couches faced each other. There was a large palm tree in a polished bronze pot. On the far side of the room was what appeared to be a long desk. On the wall behind the desk were a number of small, mysterious cubicles. She watched Ring walk up to the desk and speak to the man behind it.

"I'm Ring Crossman," he said politely. "I'm looking for my hand, Rowdy Hayes."

"Oh, yes, Mr. Crossman, I remember you. Glad to have you back, sir. But Mr. Hayes isn't here just now. I believe he's at the restaurant."

"That's a good place for him to be. I'm hungry enough t'eat my saddle." Ring tipped his hat to the clerk and turned to leave. "Oh, I'm sorry. Blaze, would you like to go on up to our rooms and do, well, whatever it is ladies do?"

Blaze quickly shook her head. The last thing she wanted to do was be alone in this place without Ring or Sandy.

"Thanks, but I'll . . . I'll come with you."

Ring smiled. "After you." He gestured to the door. Blaze couldn't leave fast enough.

Back in the street, Ring headed in a familiar direction. Blaze walked just behind him while Sandy limped along in the rear. Blaze saw Ring start, then lift his hand in greeting.

"Rowdy. Good to see you."

A stooped, older man with long, snow-white hair raised a hand almost imperceptibly by way of reply. His deeply lined face remained sober. Blaze glanced at Sandy.

"Don't pay Rowdy no mind, Miss Blaze. He looks like 'at all the time."

Blaze wasn't so sure. She kept her eyes on Ring, who seemed to tense all of a sudden.

"What is it, Rowdy?" Ring asked, confirming Blaze's suspicion. "What's wrong?"

Rowdy inclined his head to a place somewhere behind him. "Let's go over t'Miss Maggie's, have a drink." Without another word, he turned and headed back up the street.

"There really must be somethin' wrong," Sandy said to Blaze. "That's the most I heard him talk since

I knowed him."

Blaze's stomach constricted. She hurried after Ring.

Maggie's saloon was another eye-opener for Blaze. A place to go and eat was wonder enough. But a place to drink?

She accepted a glass of water only when Ring asked her what she wanted. He bought beer for everyone else. They took their drinks to a round table and sat down. Blaze wrinkled her nose at the smell of the alcohol, then promptly forgot about everything but Ring. He had gone pale.

"Better tell me what it is, Rowdy," he said tightly. "I'd sure like to get over to see my mother."

Rowdy didn't reply. He looked at Ring without blinking.

"Unless, of course, it's about my mother."

Rowdy held Ring's gaze for another long moment. His pallor deepened.

"I'm sorry, Ring," Rowdy said quietly. "I'm sure as hell sorry."

There was another long, painful silence. Then: "Did she suffer?"

"She was sick a long time, Ring," Rowdy said soberly. "She passed in 'er sleep. It was a blessin'."

Ring nodded slowly and stared down at his clasped hands. "How long ago?" he asked without looking up.

"Near a month," Rowdy replied. "It was a real nice funeral, Ring. I did the best I could."

Ring nodded again. "Thanks, Rowdy. I appreciate it."

Blaze felt a tear slip down her cheek.

"Guess I'll go on over to her house, then." Ring got up and walked toward the double swinging doors.

Heart breaking, Blaze followed.

CHAPTER EIGHT

THE SOUND OF MOURNING DOVES CAME THROUGH THE open window, carried on the wings of a fresh, spring breeze. The gauzy curtains fluttered and settled, fluttered and settled, as if breathing in and out. Drowsing beneath the colorful quilt, Blaze inhaled the desert perfume of blooming cacti, and the lingering scent of night-blooming jasmine that Ring's mother, Priscilla Wade, had planted in her backyard garden.

She would have to get up soon. Rowdy, Ring, and Sandy would be by for their breakfast. Blaze smiled to herself.

Ring hadn't wanted her to do that for them. At least that's what he said. But she knew he was secretly delighted. As were Sandy and Rowdy. Her mother had taught her well, and they liked her cooking. Blaze giggled.

Rowdy absolutely hated to cook, yet earned his living that way. Maybe that's what made him so grumpy all the time.

The pink light of dawn stole through the window to stain the simple, white-painted dresser and warm the quilt Blaze had pulled to her chin. She closed her eyes and still saw the comforting light. She'd cook, then have her lesson on her very own horse.

Blaze shivered with pleasure. Her own horse. The most beautiful animal she had ever seen. Purest white with a sprinkling of black spots over his rump and a funny black circle around his left eye. He had a funny expression, too. He'd hang his head a little, let his ears flop, and look at her with those big, brown eyes. With the black ring especially, he looked so pitiful, kind of lonesome. It had taken her awhile to think of just the right name. Then it had seemed obvious.

Lonesome. She'd call him Lonesome. Not only did he appear that way, but it was a talisman of sorts. Neither one of them would ever be lonely again.

Blaze hugged her arms to her breast. She had always thought she would love to have a horse. What she hadn't imagined was how much she was going to love the horse itself.

Thinking about Lonesome brought her naturally to thoughts of Ring. Blaze experienced a feeling of warmth that spread outward from the center of her breast. Could it be from her heart, she wondered. She recalled that fateful day nearly three months ago.

Ring had walked straight to the cemetery. It had been painful to watch him search for her grave. Row after row he walked until he found it at last. He knelt on one knee. His chin dropped to his chest.

Blaze had watched from a distance, and was glad she had when a sob escaped her. She realized her face was wet with tears. Her heart ached for Ring.

He had remained kneeling for a very long time. Once Blaze saw him lift a hand to his eyes and scrub them. She herself never moved a muscle.

She was not certain how long she had stood at the cemetery's edge, watching him. What seemed an eternity later, however, he rose and walked slowly back to the cemetery's entrance, head down. When he passed her, he looked up and appeared surprised.

"You're here." It was a simple statement of fact, yet it contained almost more meaning and emotion than Blaze could bear.

"Yes. I'm here," she replied with equal simplicity.

Ring nodded. "Thank you."

"Would you like to show me your mother's house?" Blaze didn't know where the words had come from, but she instantly sensed they were the exact right ones.

A small, sad smile touched Ring's lips. "I'd like that very much."

They walked down the main street side by side, silent. At the opposite edge of town, Ring turned right down a narrow street lined with small, quaint stores. When the row of stores came to an end, he kept walking. Blaze saw, in the distance, a neat, white clapboard house surrounded by a white picket fence and tidy gardens, front and back. She glanced at Ring.

There was another smile on his mouth, but this one was only vaguely tinged with sadness. Blaze felt her spirits lift a little. At the front entrance to the house, Ring opened a low gate and held it for her. She stepped into the magical enclosure of Priscilla Wade's home.

Flowers, sadly wilting now from lack of care, grew against the sides of the house. There was a front porch with a rocker off to one side, and lace curtains on the windows at either side of the front door. Overwhelmed, Blaze followed Ring onto the front porch. Again he held the door for her, and she stepped inside. She heard the door close behind her.

"It's not much, I know," she heard Ring say. "But my mother loved it."

"Not much?" Blaze turned to Ring. Her eyebrows had nearly disappeared into her hairline. "I think it's the most beautiful home I've ever seen."

Ring was silent for a moment. He swallowed. "Would you like me to . . . to show you around?"

Blaze could only nod. Ring gestured around them.

"My mother's parlor," he said needlessly.

It was charming. There was another rocking chair in one corner, facing a settee, with a small, low table between them. In another corner was a knickknack shelf, filled with figurines and pretty rocks.

"I found those, and gave them to her when I was just a kid," Ring said as if he had read her mind.

Something hard and uncomfortable formed in Blaze's chest. She was glad of the room's cheery colors; pinks and blues, a soft, pale green.

Ring led her on to the next room, the kitchen. Lace hung at the windows here as well. A real sink with water pump and a cast-iron stove. Cups in a pretty blue and white pattern hung under cabinets on one wall. Behind one glass cupboard door she saw matching saucers and plates. There was a small, square oaken table in the center of the room with four matching chairs.

"Oh, Ring," Blaze sighed. "I . . . I don't know what to say. It's wonderful."

"Let me show you your room," he said by way of reply.

It was as if Blaze had suddenly become numb. It simply didn't register. *Her room?* She followed Ring back through the salon and through a door off to one side.

The bedroom looked as if it had been decorated for

the princess in a story her mother had read to her when she was a little girl. The curtains at the window were gauzy and reached all the way to the pine floor. The quilt on the bed was in pastel colors. A small table, bearing a lamp, stood beside it. A matching dresser graced the opposite wall. Blaze was speechless.

"Do you like it?" Ring asked finally.

Blaze thought she nodded, but wasn't sure.

"So, you won't mind staying here?"

Blaze came to her senses at last. She turned to him. "Oh, Ring, I couldn't. I just couldn't."

"Why not?"

"Well, it's . . . it's . . . so *grand*."

A smile almost made it to his lips. "Blaze, my mother wasn't grand. She was a solid, decent, loving woman. She would have wanted you to stay here. She would have insisted on it, in fact. You two had a great deal in common."

Blaze was astounded. "Your mother and . . . me?"

"You're the two strongest women I ever knew."

Blaze was speechless.

"Would you come and sit on the porch with me for awhile, Blaze? I'd like to tell you how I got my name."

"Of course I'll sit with you," she replied in a small voice.

Ring took the rocker from the parlor and put it near the one on the porch. They sat down side by side.

"My mother was a schoolteacher," Ring began. "She taught at a small school outside St. Louis, Missouri. One day a young man came riding by. It was a hot day, and he was thirsty, so he came inside to ask for a drink of water." Ring leaned forward, elbows on his knees. "He was a handsome man, powerfully good lookin'. When he left, my mother thought she would never see him again. She was wrong.

"He came back the next day and asked for a drink of water. And the next day, and the next. Then one afternoon, when school was out, he asked if he might take her for a walk."

Blaze stared at Ring with rapt attention. His gaze was focused somewhere out over the far horizon.

"He came every afternoon for a month, and they walked out together. Then he asked her to marry him."

Vaguely, Blaze remembered Ring's mother's last name was different from his. "Did she accept?" she breathed.

"Yes. She did. She adored him."

Blaze's brow wrinkled in puzzlement. "So, they went away together and got married?"

"Well, they went away together. Joseph, my daddy, had always wanted to move to the southwest. My mother was willing to go, but wanted to be married first. He promised they'd get hitched as soon as they got to Arizona."

"But that didn't happen, did it?"

Ring shook his head. "He got her a real nice little house, this one, and took a job at the livery stable. Then Ma got pregnant."

Blaze raised a hand to her mouth. Ring didn't even seem to notice her.

"She thought then, for sure," he continued, "that my daddy would marry her. She was so sure that she decided to name her baby, whether it was a girl or a boy . . . Ring. She was convinced that a baby was what was gonna finally put that ring on her finger." Ring sighed heavily.

"So, that's what she did when I was born. She even gave me my daddy's last name. It didn't do her a bit of good."

Blaze felt tears well in her eyes.

"A week after I was born, he just didn't . . . he just didn't come home one day. My mother never saw him again." Ring stared at the distant mountains for a long moment, then cleared his throat.

"But she raised me right, took over my daddy's job at the livery, and sent me to school."

"The livery? But . . . she was a teacher, Ring."

He was silent. "She had a child out of wedlock," he said at length in a dull tone. "The town shunned her. She was lucky to get a job cleaning stalls." Ring stood and walked slowly down the porch steps.

"Ring? Wait. Please."

Blaze started to follow, but he spoke without stopping or turning.

"I'm going back to the cemetery for awhile. You stay here, get settled in. I'll see you later."

The sun was over the horizon. It poured through the window like warm honey. Blaze knew it was time to get up and get going. But she lingered just a moment longer.

She had stayed in Priscilla's house, of course. Blaze had told Ring it was only until the snow melted in the mountains and she could continue her way north. She didn't tell him why. He didn't ask. He told her simply to move on in.

So she had, and the past months had been filled with a quiet joy. She had her horse, as Ring had promised. She rode every day. She lived in a beautiful house. And there was Ring's company, always pleasant.

She had such warm feelings for Ring. He was a kind man, and treated her like a lady. Those were two things her mother had always told her she loved about Blaze's father. Did she love Ring? Blaze rolled over onto her side.

How could she know? She had never been in love

before. And she had imagined something different when she did fall in love.

And then there was her mission. Nothing, no one, could stop her. Would he join her? Would he want to?

Blaze moaned. What was she going to do? How was she going to know if she was in love or not?

She threw her legs over the edge of the bed. To heck with her lesson. She was going to ask Ring if he would ride out into the desert with her instead. What she was going to do when they got there, she didn't know. But she would think of something. She was sure she would.

Blaze just knew she had to go.

CHAPTER NINE

BLAZE DIDN'T THINK SHE HAD EVER SEEN THE DESERT look so beautiful. Large yellow blooms decorated the prickly pear, smaller ones dusted the leafless paloverde. Pink blossoms erupted on the barrel cacti, while sage and mesquite bloomed with tiny yellow flowers. Red-petaled blooms decorated the long, spiny arms of the ocotillo. Due to recent rains, here and there on the valley floor were sparse patches of grass, thin and fine as a baby's hair. The desert was alive and wearing its spring finery.

The sweet scents and stirring beauty were a balm to Blaze's soul. Although the terrible tragedy in her life, the pain and loss, never left her, for this moment at least she felt light of heart. The feeling helped warm her for the task she had set for herself. Blaze glanced toward the man riding at her side.

She loved the way Ring sat a horse. He seemed so

at home, so easy in the saddle. His back was straight, but not rigid, giving him the appearance of flowing along with his horse instead of merely riding it. His hands held the reins loosely, and his eyes were heavy lidded beneath the wide brim of his Stetson. But Blaze was not fooled. He was like a snake sleeping in the sun. In the space of a heartbeat he could be tensed to strike. She smiled to herself.

There were so many things she liked about Ring Crossman. She'd been right to come out with him like this today. Her instincts had been correct. If there could ever be anything between them, she would find out now. The thought of her single-minded mission did not even distress her. What was meant to be, would be.

The pair had ridden for some time at a slow, but ground-eating lope. Blaze had enjoyed every moment of her horse's rocking chair gait, and was reluctant to stop. But they had ridden quite a way out into the desert and it would be time to turn back soon. It was more than time she speak to Ring about what was on her mind.

His first clue had been when she declined a lesson and suggested they ride out together. It wasn't that he thought her idea odd. Rather, it was the way she acted when she asked him. Ring glanced sidelong at Blaze and shook his head.

She was a strange one, all right. All sealed up tight around a core of something hard and terrible, something, he had to admit, he might never know about. Something that was driving, or pushing her north. She was on a quest of some kind. Or a hunt.

Ring felt the hair on his arms stand up as he recalled how coolly she had informed him she had killed a man. She was no stranger to death and dying. That much he was certain of. What puzzled him was the other side of her, the side that flourished despite whatever it was she had gone through. The part of her that made him want to take her in his arms and make the rest of her world go away. He stole another look at the woman who rode beside him when she slowed her horse to a walk.

There was something on her mind. He'd known her long enough and well enough to figure that much out. She wanted to talk to him. But about what? Ring's stomach suddenly spasmed.

Was it time for her to move on? The snow had started to melt in the mountains. Is that what she wanted to tell him? In the next moment, his worst fears were realized.

Blaze halted her gelding abruptly and looked Ring

straight in the eye. There was no other way to go at it, she decided, except straight.

"I . . . I want you to know, Ring," Blaze began, "that it was . . . special . . . staying in your mother's house. You've been very kind to me. And I can never thank you enough for Lonesome." Unconsciously, her hand stroked the spotted horse's neck. "But it's about time I . . . I thought about heading north again."

Ring felt cold. His response was merely a curt nod.

Blaze felt distinctly uneasy. This was harder than she had thought, and Ring wasn't helping. She loosened her reins and let Lonesome walk on. Her gaze focused on a small homestead in the near distance, but she didn't really see it.

"I was . . . thinking," she continued unsteadily. "Wondering, really, if you . . . I mean . . . if you and I might be heading in kind of . . . well . . . the same direction."

Ring's heart normally didn't skip many beats. He had to swallow to try to regain his composure.

"Well, you know I . . . I like to take my horses to Westport and sell 'em to the folks headed west. So, I guess I'm headed to Missouri. You haven't told me much about where you're goin', except north."

It was true. And it troubled her. Blaze's brow wrinkled into furrows.

"Truth is," she admitted, "I'm not exactly sure

where I'm headed. Except north."

Ring decided to take a big risk. If she was thinking what he hoped . . . prayed . . . she was thinking, he wanted to be able to help her in any way he could.

"Are you sure the person, or people, you're looking for aren't around these parts any longer?"

Blaze looked at Ring sharply. Her hands tightened on the reins, and Lonesome stopped.

"What do you know about who I'm looking for?" she asked tensely. A scowl hovered on her brow.

With effort, Ring remained perfectly calm. "Nothing. Absolutely nothing. It was just a guess, Blaze."

She tried not to let it, but the pain welled up in her. She looked away from Ring, toward the small house in the distance.

Ring cursed himself silently. He had spoiled the moment. He hoped he hadn't ruined his entire future as well.

"I'm sorry," he apologized quietly. "I sure didn't mean to stir up any bad feelings. That's the last thing I'd want to have happen between us . . . bad feelings."

Blaze bit her lip to try to focus on a different pain. She tried to recall the warmth she had felt earlier, the wonder of the emotion she had thought she had felt for Ring. But there was now only a bleak chill in her breast, and she felt terrible. She had seen clearly in Ring's eyes, in his expression, how he would have responded to her suggestion they travel together.

"I don't . . . I don't have any bad feelings toward you, Ring," Blaze forced herself to say at last. "There's just something I . . . I have to do."

"You don't have to do it alone, Blaze," Ring heard himself saying.

She closed her eyes and took a deep breath. *Please let the feelings come back*, Blaze prayed. *Whatever they were, please let them come back.*

But her heart remained hard, filled only with the dreadful purpose that had consumed her life. And she knew, without doubt, that what she felt for Ring was simply the ease and comfort of friendship, a talisman against the dark of night, a barrier to loneliness. She touched her horse's neck once again. Blaze sighed.

She had wanted to love him. He was a good man. But he wasn't the right man.

"Ring, I . . . I have to say something. I . . ."

He held up a restraining hand. She thought it was because he didn't want to hear what she had to say, but in the next moment she heard what had caught his attention. And saw the dust cloud swirl about the little house.

"Looks like there might be trouble," Ring said needlessly. "Maybe you'd better ride back and let me . . ."

She was gone before he could finish his sentence, responding just as he had feared she would. He put his heels to his bay mare with the hope of merely catching up with her.

Lonesome was a sturdy animal, trail wise and patient. And fast. Blaze was grateful for his fleetness of foot when another scream, a woman's scream, tore straight into her heart. She leaned a little lower over her horse's neck.

The house was small, built as it was of rare and precious lumber. The back of the structure was shaded by a generous paloverde, and beyond the tree were half a dozen acres that appeared to have been recently put to the plow. A man in a farmer's simple garb sat astride a shaggy, solidly built horse and futilely brandished a rifle at a small band of mounted braves. He had placed himself between the Indians and a woman and child who huddled against the side of the house. Laughing and whooping, the mounted men reached around the farmer to jab their guns at his hapless family.

Something hard and horrible rose up in Blaze. There was a strange, metallic taste in her mouth. Her breathing was rapid and shallow. Her teeth were clenched so hard a tic jumped in her jaw, and her hands clutched so tightly on the reins her fingernails dug into her flesh. She heard shouting, but was unable to recognize words. She rode down on the braves as hard and fast as she was able.

There was but one thought in her mind. *Save them.*

Ring's fear was all for Blaze. *Hotheaded little fool*, he silently railed. What had gotten into her? Didn't she know better than to charge into the midst of a band of riled-up renegade Indians? He lashed the end of his reins across his mare's flanks, then reached down for the ever-present rifle in its sheath. It was never a good idea to bring out a weapon in a situation like this, but it didn't look like Blaze's attack was going to leave him any choice. She was going for it wholeheartedly.

With a kind of horrified fascination, Ring watched Blaze ride, full tilt, into the center of the group. The swiftness and headlong nature of her charge seemed to take them by surprise and, as she rode through the middle of them, they drew back, scattering as they wheeled their horses out of the way. Seconds later, Ring had reached the house, rifle leveled at first one, then another of the braves.

"Don't anybody move," he said tightly. Then wondered what in the hell he was going to do next. The brave nearest him, Apache by his dress, openly sneered.

"Or what, white man?"

Ring swung his rifle toward the man who had spoken. What a damn, stupid mess to get into, he thought. What a damn, stupid way to die. His next thought was that he had never seen a human being move so fast.

Blaze had ridden out, Ring knew, without her guns. He considered her, therefore, weaponless. He couldn't have been more wrong. Like the lightning he had named her for, she struck out in three directions all at once, a pure force of stunning energy.

The rider closest to her, on the right, surrendered his rifle without a fuss. She was simply too quick, and he was totally unprepared. She snatched it, and in the same, sweeping motion, brought the weapon around to her left and caught another rider with a sharp blow on his right shoulder. At the same moment she kicked out her left leg, catching the brave's horse in the ribs. The horse bolted and his rider, unbalanced by the blow, tumbled to the ground. He hit the hard dirt with a grunt, and his rifle spun away from him. Ring jumped from his horse and grabbed it.

In the space of seconds, two of the four braves had been disarmed. Ring realized he and Blaze now held three weapons to their two. In spite of himself, he grinned. It acted like a signal to the farmer, who leapt from his horse, grabbed his wife and daughter, and shoved them through the front door of the little house. The two Indians who remained armed were galvanized.

"Shit," Ring breathed as he watched the man with a four-fingered hand raise his rifle to his shoulder and aim at Blaze. His finger tightened on his trigger. "Shoot her and you're a dead man," he hissed.

"And I will be the one who will kill you."

All eyes swiveled toward the man who ridden up, totally unnoticed, and spoken. Ring heard Blaze draw in her breath.

"Put down your weapons. All of you." The man's voice was deep. Commanding. Ring noted that the braves obeyed at once. To Ring's amazement, so did Blaze. Slowly, reluctantly, he lowered his weapon as well.

"What has happened here?" the man asked. His horse danced sideways, and he controlled the mare with no visible effort. "You." He indicated the farmer. "Speak to me."

The farmer glanced around him warily. He removed his straw hat and turned it nervously in his fingers.

"We . . . we would have given them food," he replied at length, haltingly. "They only needed to ask. They . . . they didn't have to try to steal it, or . . . or torment my wife and daughter."

The man who questioned the farmer was tall, his skin browned by the sun, his waist-length hair blue-black. His beaded shirt and leggings were distinctly Apache. But his eyes were blue. Sky blue and piercing. They narrowed as his brow furrowed.

"Chinalgo," he said to the four-fingered man. "Go. Take these women with you." He indicated the three other braves. "I will deal with them later."

For long moments the only sound was of hoof-beats. The four Apache braves disappeared in a trailing cloud of dust. The tall man turned his searing gaze on Blaze.

"You have courage. And cunning. These people owe you their thanks."

"Yes, ma'am." The farmer nodded vigorously, still twisting his hat. His wife and daughter peered through the partially open door behind him. "Thank you. Thank you very much. Both of you."

Ring felt an unfamiliar heat rise to his face. He nodded briefly, aware that the tall man barely glanced at him.

"Is he your . . . mate?" the man asked Blaze abruptly.

"No."

"Tell me your name."

"Blaze," she replied without hesitation. Ring thought he saw the tinge of a smile touch the corners of her mouth. "And yours?"

The tall man was silent for the span of several seconds. Ring noticed something happen at the corners of his mouth as well.

"My people have named me Baa hilzaa n'ii idi'dii."

Blaze's smile blossomed full. "Bringer of Thunder," she said confidently.

The tall man showed very white and even teeth.

"You know my people's language."

"Not by choice." Blaze's smile vanished as quickly as it had appeared. "But by necessity. Many of *my* people had to learn to beg for their lives in the language of their enemy."

The tall man's smile lessened, but did not depart. He nodded slowly. His horse shook its head and snorted.

"You are a worthy adversary, Blaze," he said, as if testing the word. "In many different ways."

The two eyed each other for another impossibly long minute. Ring could almost feel, physically, the tension between them. He wanted to get back on his horse but was, unaccountably, afraid to move. He wasn't sure what it was, but something was happening. Instinct warned him to keep perfectly still.

"On behalf of my people, I apologize," the tall man said at last to the farmer. "Like many young men, even white men, they forget their manners from time to time." He returned his hard, bright stare to Blaze. "I apologize to you as well, Blaze. And to your companion." He reined his horse around, obviously preparing to ride away.

"Wait."

The tall man turned in his saddle.

"You told me your name," Blaze said in a curious tone of voice. "But you didn't tell me what they call you."

The brilliant smile reappeared. His horse trotted in

place, eager to go, while the tall man held him in check. "As I said, you are cunning." He laughed, the sound like a short bark. His horse reared, standing briefly on two legs. "Bane," he called out as his mount's front feet touched the ground again. He gave the animal its head, and the horse burst into a ground-devouring run.

"Bane," Ring repeated with a shake of his head. "Bane of the white man, I suppose he means."

Blaze ignored him. She tossed the captured rifle to the farmer. "You'd better keep this," she said. "You never know when you might need it." Without another word, she turned and rode away.

Ring caught up with her quickly. He felt strange, as if he'd just awoken from a dream. "We were damn lucky," he commented at length. "That episode could've ended pretty badly. Fortunately, that . . . Bane . . . turned out to be an honorable man."

"He's a dangerous man."

Ring looked over at Blaze sharply. "What?"

"He's a dangerous man," Blaze repeated. Her expression seemed distant, focused on something very far away. "Something is burning inside of him, consuming him."

Ring was totally perplexed. "How . . . how could you know that?"

Blaze reined her horse to a stop and looked Ring straight in the eye. "Because I recognize it," she said, so softly he barely heard. And then she was gone, galloping away from him as rapidly as the tall man had taken flight.

Ring started to follow, but let his mare fall out of the lope almost at once. With slowly dawning realization, and heavy heart, he knew that Blaze had done more than just ride away from him.

She had ridden out of his life.

CHAPTER TEN

FOR THE NEXT FEW DAYS, BLAZE MOVED AS IF WITHIN the confines of a dream. The incident with the farmer and his family had an air of unreality about it. Trying to catch and hold on to the memory was like attempting to cling to the fringe of a cloud. First there had been shock and rage for the family's plight, then the frenzy of action. She had done things she had not ever dreamed she could do. And then the tall man had come. The tall man with the light eyes.

Blaze's dreamlike haziness intensified. Bane, he had called himself. Bane to the white man. Bringer of Thunder to the Apache. But who was he, truly? Where had he come from? And to whose people did he really belong? He led Apaches, yet had protected the whites. Staring straight ahead, lost in her thoughts, Blaze tripped over a rock partially hidden in the dusty street. She returned abruptly to the present and looked about her.

She had almost reached the livery. She wondered if Ring would have time for her today. Probably not, she thought. He was busy putting the final touches on the horses he had trained over the winter. They would leave any day now. And she had told Ring she would leave with them, ride along with them. At least until she picked up the trail she sought. Blaze sighed heavily.

Everything was different now. Painfully different. Blaze suspected Ring knew why she had asked him to ride out into the desert with her. She was sure he knew exactly what she had been on the verge of revealing to him. She most certainly knew the sadness he felt since that day. Most troubling of all, however, was her inability to understand just what had happened to her. She had started the day wondering if she might be falling in love with Ring Crossman. She had ended it knowing he was not, and would never be, the man for her. What had changed so dramatically? And why did she become so irritatingly restless each time she thought about it?

Fleeing from it yet again, Blaze closed the distance to the livery and rounded the side of the barn. The corrals were busy, as she had envisioned. Sandy caught sight of her and waved.

"Hey, Blaze."

Blaze smiled at him. He walked with only a slight limp, a fact for which she was profoundly grateful. As was Sandy, and his puppy-like devotion was often disconcerting.

"You want me t'saddle up Lonesome, Miss Blaze?"

"Thanks, Sandy. I'll get him." She walked past the first corral, where the activity was taking place, to a smaller paddock where they kept their personal riding stock. Ring nodded at Blaze as she passed.

"Sorry, but I'm a little tied up today. No pun intended," he added, and hefted the rope he had coiled over his arm.

He smiled, but it was a sad smile, Blaze thought. "Do you need me to help?"

He shook his head. "As long as you intend to fry up that steak you promised me this mornin', you take your horse and enjoy yourself for awhile."

Blaze felt a little guilty, riding out while the others worked. But she did her share feeding them twice a day, which freed Rowdy up to help. Besides, their roles would be reversed on the trail, with Rowdy cooking and her tailing horses. And she felt like a ride today. A ride alone, just her and Lonesome.

The big, spotted horse regarded her patiently. Nary an ear twitched when she threw her saddle on his back and cinched him up tightly. He held his head low, as if aiding her, when she slipped on his bridle.

Blaze led him out of the corral and mounted.

Sandy waved as she passed. Ring's gaze followed her solemnly. Rowdy ignored her entirely. She kicked Lonesome into a jog when they rounded the corner of the barn.

Many of the people in the street looked at her strangely. She had become used to it. There were not many women who rode about in men's clothing. Fewer still with waist-length black hair creased by lightning. Self-consciously, Blaze raised a hand to her temple.

She couldn't feel it, and seldom thought about it. Only an occasional mirror brought her up short. Did Bane remember it? Did he remember *her*?

The mere idea caused her to squirm in her saddle. An instant later it made her angry.

What was she doing thinking about the leader of a ragtag band of renegade Apaches anyway? She was never even going to see him again.

Unconsciously, Blaze put her heels to her horse's sides and he broke into a lope. They galloped away from the town, keeping to the road until the shadow of Squaw Peak fell across their way. Blaze reined to a walk and looked up at the small mountain.

She and Ring had once ridden up the narrow trail that wound near to the top. The view of the dry, sun-drenched valley below had been breathtaking. She considered riding up there again. It might be her last look, for a very long time, at the southern deserts that had so long been her home.

Lonesome was trail wise and sure-footed. He picked his way slowly up the narrow, rocky path. Lizards sunning on slate-colored rocks scurried for cover. Tufts of hardy grass poked from crevices, and once, faintly, Blaze heard the warning trill of a rattler. A hawk soared high overhead.

The sun was warm on her back and neck and, although the steep, winding path grew more narrow, Blaze had every confidence in her horse. She relaxed into her saddle, wrists crossed over the pommel, shoulders slightly slumped. Her eyelids felt heavy, and she glanced at the desert beauty all around her with a certain serenity. In the distant recesses of her mind, she retained the knowledge that these might be her last peaceful moments. There was a long, hard road ahead, and a bloody one. Her journey would not be over until vengeance was fulfilled.

High above, the circling hawk suddenly screamed. Blaze jerked upright, instantly alert. Lonesome's ears pricked forward and he stopped.

The hawk had sighted something, not prey, but an enemy, or an intruder. The hairs on the back of Blaze's arms stood up, and she knew, with certainty, that she was not alone. But where could someone, or some*thing* be hiding?

Blaze looked around her, but there was only rock climbing up and away to her left, and falling away downward to her right. The trail wound up and around to the left, spiraling toward the peak. She couldn't see around the corner, but doubted anyone could hide there. From experience, she knew that the trail narrowed and rose to a sharp degree no horse could safely negotiate, especially so high up. One false step meant certain death. A lone person, however, or some lithe desert creature, might make it all the way to the top. Did something await her around the bend?

Blaze's heart beat a little faster. This was the point where she had to turn around. Lonesome could not go any farther. It was time to head back anyway. In another couple of hours Ring and his crew would be coming by the house for their supper. She should turn around now and go.

But curiosity held her in a grip she could not loosen. Not only was she armed, she sensed no danger from whatever was ahead. Slowly, very carefully, she dismounted. Her foot dislodged a loose rock, and it bounced out of sight down the side of the mountain. She edged around in front of her horse.

The trail narrowed to barely the width of her stance. It also became extremely steep, forcing her to scrabble upward on all fours. As she rounded the corner, she was able to stand again, and gratefully straightened her spine. She found herself face to face with the man who called himself Bane.

A strange thrill ran through Blaze, a wave of warmth that washed over her and left her skin prickling with excitement when it withdrew. But it was wrong. So wrong. Blaze took an involuntary step backward.

A strong, brown, long-fingered hand fastened around her wrist. A bolt of fear shot through her heart, until she felt the ground begin to crumble beneath her right foot. She was too close to the edge; the trail was giving way. She was going to fall off the side of the mountain. Fear turned into the full shock of panic. But Bane had known she was in danger. Thank God he had grabbed her wrist. He drew her forward until she stood on solid footing once more.

"Thank . . . thank you," she whispered.

He regarded her silently, a faint smile on his thin but handsome mouth. His eyes were startlingly bright above the high, sharp planes of his cheekbones.

"How have you come to this high place?" he asked Blaze at length.

"I rode," she replied simply.

"Yes. I saw, and heard, you coming. But why?"

It seemed a strange question to ask. But then the whole situation was odd. The dreamlike quality she had experienced the last few days settled over her again. This time, however, it wrapped her tightly. She knew she could not escape, could not return down the mountain, even if she wished. This was a scene that had been written before, and now must be played out.

"Why?" Bane repeated. "Why come, alone, to the eagle's peak?"

Why, indeed? She felt, somehow, he already knew. Certainly, he would know if she did not tell him the truth.

"I came to look on the land that has been my home," she said at last. "Probably for the last time."

Bane nodded slowly, as if considering her words. "Yet, you come from the high desert south of here. You knew my name, understood the language of my mother's people, who live below the Gila River."

His "mother's people." So. "Yes. My village was to the south."

"'Was?'"

Blaze remained perfectly still. She knew she had not given herself away by so much as the flicker of an eyelash. Yet he knew.

"So that is the fire that burns in you. Vengeance."

She seemed to sink deeper into the dream. Even the edges of her vision became blurry, indistinct. She looked deeply into his light blue eyes and saw herself reflected.

"As it is with me, so it is with you," Blaze said in a voice she barely recognized. "You are burned by the same fire."

His expression never altered. His vague smile remained fixed in place. "There is no heaven for people like us," he said finally. "Only hell."

"Does it matter?" Blaze thought she heard him laugh softly, but couldn't be sure. A long silence stretched between them. She did not find it uncomfortable. On the contrary, it seemed a natural part of the dream.

"You leave soon," Bane said eventually, conversationally. "With the horseman."

"I'm traveling north with him, yes."

Once again, Bane nodded slowly. "So, your path leads you to the north. Are you sure of it?"

How much did he actually know? Blaze wondered. And how much did he surmise?

"I know that the people I seek are no longer in the southern deserts. My journey will begin simply by leaving here."

Another span of moments spread between them. Bane rose from the edge of a rock on which he had perched.

"People who wish to see far come to this peak," he said enigmatically. "They are few. And they are often lonely."

His light eyes bored into her. An early evening breeze lifted the long, black hair from his shoulders.

"We must go. Shadows will increase the danger

of the trail."

With a start, Blaze realized how low the sun had set. She started back toward Lonesome, then looked over her shoulder.

"I have my horse, and you're on foot. Would you—"

Bane shook his head, interrupting her. He made a small sound with his tongue and lips.

Blaze would not have believed it if she had not seen it herself. From behind Bane, higher up on the trail, almost from the top, his black mare appeared. She bobbed her head, and her long, thick mane lifted from her neck. Her small, delicate hooves placed themselves confidently on the loose rock.

There was nothing to say. It was simply an extension of the fantastic dream. Blaze walked down to her horse, squeezed by him next to the cliffside, and mounted handily. At her command, Lonesome turned in place until he was headed down the trail. She looked back and saw Bane follow. When he had reached a wider, more level part of the path, he waited for his mare. She came up next to him, and he swung onto her back with no apparent effort. Blaze squeezed her legs, and Lonesome started downward.

Not a word was spoken all the way down from the peak. The only sounds were of hooves on the trail, and loose rock slipping down the mountainside. Shadows were long by the time they reached the desert floor.

Lonesome trotted a step, as if glad to be off the steep, narrow trail. He stopped and briefly laid back his ears as the black mare drew even with him. Blaze looked at Bane and simply waited for the next part of the dream to unfold.

The setting sun cast a pinkish glow about them both. Failing light hid their expressions from one another. Then Bane lifted a hand to his forehead, as if in some silent salute. He wheeled his mare and galloped away to the west.

When the hoofbeats faded, Blaze turned her horse to the north. Unbidden, Lonesome broke into a lope. Moving into the night wind, she never felt the tears that streaked her cheeks.

CHAPTER ELEVEN

THERE WAS NOTHING MORE BLAZE COULD DO IN THE small, tidy house. She had rendered it spotlessly clean, and eliminated all signs of her habitation. The home looked exactly as it had when she first entered it during the winter. Blaze sighed.

She did not leave this place happily. She had enjoyed greater comfort here than she had ever known in her life. Ring had been more than kind to her, and she had loved Sandy's lighthearted company. Even Rowdy had grown on her. She walked slowly to the front doors and picked up her bedroll.

Sandy had shown her how to pack up efficiently. Within the bedroll were a few personal possessions; changes of clothing, a hairbrush, soap, and a sliver of mirror. It was fastened tightly with rawhide thongs and would fit over Lonesome's back behind her saddle.

Blaze walked out onto the front porch and closed the door behind her.

She didn't lock it. Mrs. Rainey, an old friend of Ring's mother, had promised to watch the house. Blaze walked away and did not look back.

Blaze walked swiftly to the livery, not with anticipation, but determination. But she ran into Ring and Rowdy in front of the general store. They were loading supplies into the back of the cook wagon. Ring eyed her as she set her bedroll on the ground beside her.

"We're not leavin' 'til the morning," he said.

"I know. I have something I need to do first. Somewhere I have to go."

Ring's eyebrows lifted a fraction. "Will you be . . . coming back?"

"I certainly plan on it. There are just some people I have to see, some questions I have to ask. If I'm not back by tomorrow morning, I'll catch up with you."

"We'll be taking the same trail up we followed comin' down. Might even stay a night in your old . . . 'homestead'."

Ring smiled and Blaze managed an answering one. The "homestead," as he called it, seemed very far away, both in time and distance.

"Well, I guess I'll see you some time tomorrow. Tell Sandy I'll see him, too."

Ring nodded. Rowdy's eyes flitted briefly in her

direction. Blaze picked up her bedroll and walked on to the livery.

The Gila River crossing was the first place she had heard word of the men who had massacred her family and the people of her village. When she had left, after burying everyone she had ever known or loved, she had walked into the mountains, either to heal or die. When her strength had returned, she crept into a farmer's crude hut one night, and stole a shirt, trousers, and a pair of sandals. Then she had walked north.

In the early days, Blaze had hidden when riders approached. She was a woman, alone and unarmed. For although she had her father's rifle, she had very little ammunition. If anyone had meant her ill, she would not have been able to defend herself for very long. Thus it was that she spoke to no one until she had reached the river crossing.

A small settlement had sprung up on the banks of the Gila. A group of Indians, friendly to both whites and Mexicans, manned the crossing and charged a modest fee. Blaze knew that if the men she sought had come this way, the Indians would know. She was correct.

The three men who tended the ferry that day eyed her warily when she approached. At the time she had not known about the streak of white in her hair, and wondered if that might have accounted for their curious stares. It was good, perhaps, she had not known, for she had approached them boldly.

"I'm looking for some men. They hunt scalps. They kill women and children, both your brothers and mine. One of them has a scar . . . here." Blaze had slashed a line down her face. The Indians exchanged glances, and she knew then the men had gone that way. She waited for someone to answer her.

What appeared to be the oldest of the three men spoke at last. "Do you wish to cross the river?"

"Only if the men I seek crossed the river before me," she replied without hesitation.

The man who had spoken issued a grunt. But her answer apparently pleased him.

"The one with the scar crossed," he said.

"And the others?"

"The one who was their leader took sick with fever. He died. Here. The others rode away to the west."

She had had to make a decision then. But it had not been too difficult. The man with the scar had hanged her brother.

"Will you take me across?"

"There is no silver in your pocket."

Blaze thought she detected the ghost of a smile when the man said that. "You are clear-seeing," she responded. "If you see into hearts as well, you know I will return to repay you when I am able."

And so she had crossed the Gila and continued to walk northward. She had met no one else who had seen, or would admit to seeing, the man with the scar. Odd, menial jobs had kept the meat on her bones until she had come to the mountain town of Mayer. She had earned her bounty money, and run into Ring and Sandy. She was about to head northward again. But she had a debt to pay first.

The older man was still there, and he recognized her. He brought the ferry over to the north side and grunted, which, she now knew, was a sign of approval. Blaze climbed off her horse.

"I've come to repay my debt."

He took the money without counting it and put it in his pocket. "You look better than the last time I saw you."

Blaze couldn't help laughing. The man's lips never moved, but his dark eyes twinkled with mirth. Then he grew abruptly serious.

"I am glad of your return," he said somberly. "I have much to tell you."

Blaze instantly felt an icy hand clamp over her heart.

Her knees felt weak. She waited for him to continue.

"Soon after you came, we heard from a traveler of a village that had vanished. Only a mass grave was to be found."

It took every ounce of courage and determination to remain expressionless. The man's eyes narrowed, multiplying the wrinkles in his already-lined face.

"You did honor to your people," he said at last, quietly.

She was unable to respond, even to blink.

"After that, I asked many people about this man with a scar, for I knew you would return. I learned that he has spent much time to the south of here, into Mexico. It is said he once had an Apache woman, but this I do not know for certain. Our Apache brothers do not speak of him with glad hearts. He hunted their scalps, as you said. And I do not believe one of their women would have lain with him willingly."

"Have you . . . have you seen him?" Blaze forced herself to ask. Her voice sounded very small to her.

"No. And neither have any of my people. So I would tell you this."

Blaze realized she was holding her breath.

"The scarred man rides away in fear. He has made too many enemies in the land that was once his home. He will not come this way again, I think. He will go north, to the plains, where there are many more scalps to take, many more enemies to make. Although he has already, I think, made the one enemy who will kill him."

The sun hugged the rim of the horizon by the time Blaze left the Gila. The sky was aflame with crimson and gold. Somewhere nearby a coyote yipped. She put a reassuring hand on Lonesome's neck.

She would have to ride through the night, alone, but she didn't mind. She did not fear the desert. She no longer feared anything but failure.

When darkness stole away the last of the light, she walked Lonesome until a nearly full moon came up. By its glow they jogged along the road. It was curious, Blaze thought, how calm she felt. Perhaps because she knew exactly where she was going, and what she had to do. Not many people she had ever known had such firm direction in their lives.

Blaze also felt, curiously, that she had a kind of guardian angel watching over her. She felt no fear whatsoever, even alone in the darkness. It was as if someone watched over her. She could almost feel their gaze upon her.

Some high, thin clouds blew away overhead, and the winking stars added their brightness to the night. Blaze let Lonesome move into a slow lope, and rode steadily toward dawn.

CHAPTER TWELVE

THE HERD OF HORSES, TRAILED BY THE COOK WAGON, started out at first light. Ring had to resist an almost-constant urge to look behind him and see if she was coming. She had said she would catch up with them, but he couldn't help worrying. Especially the way she'd been acting recently.

A sharp whinny brought Ring back to the present. But it was only one of the mares feeling sassy in the cool dawn air. He sank back into his thoughts.

He knew from the first she would be dangerous to love. She was driven by something dark and terrible that had changed her forever. Her course would never be smooth, or simple. He had told himself that over and over again. To no avail.

Something on the trail spooked one of the horses, and he galloped ahead. The others followed, and for a minute or two Ring and Sandy had to step up their pace. The herd eventually settled back to a slower pace, and Ring drew Duchess to a jog. He looked back over his shoulder. No sign of her.

He tried to stop thinking about Blaze, but it didn't happen. Even with his eyes closed Ring could see her face before him, smooth, olive-toned skin and wide, dark, almond-shaped eyes. He touched a finger to his own lips as he recalled the full, sculpted lines of Blaze's mouth. He had once thought to feel that mouth against his.

A now-familiar sadness welled in Ring's heart. He had been so sure, that day they had ridden out into the desert, she wanted to talk to him about her feelings. Feelings he had imagined were kindly toward him. Then the incident with the farmer and the Apache braves had occurred, and everything seemed to change. After that Blaze had withdrawn into herself, almost as if the outer edges of a molten core had begun to harden. Or was it something else?

Although it gave him no pleasure, Ring could not help but remember the tall man, the half breed with the pale eyes. There was something about him, a commanding presence. And more. Something Blaze identified with. Was it something that had stolen her heart from the path he once hoped it might take?

Ring shook his head. He had to stop thinking

that way. He had enough troubles on his mind.

There was the sky up ahead, for instance. He hurried his mare's pace a notch, and caught up with Sandy.

"What do you think?" Ring jutted his chin in the direction of the clouds massing over the mountains.

"It's definitely rainin' up there," Sandy replied. "We might have trouble if we don't reach Blackjack Creek soon."

"That's what I thought." Ring found himself glancing backward one more time. "We could push the herd, get there by dark. But I'm not sure Rowdy and the wagon could keep up. Then we'd be stranded anyway."

Sandy shrugged. "It's your call, boss. We gotta think about Miss Blaze, too."

Ring wished Sandy hadn't said anything. It added substance to the worry he was already trying to ignore.

"We'll stay at our pace," he said at last. "Maybe we'll get lucky and the rains'll quit up north."

"Think positive, boss," Sandy rejoined brightly. "This ain't the time o' year fer all that rain anyhow."

"From your lips to God's ears," Ring muttered under his breath. But he didn't have a very good feeling.

By dawn Blaze was about five miles south of Phoenix, and Lonesome was tired. She was going to have to let him walk a good way. She probably wasn't going to be able to catch up with Ring and his crew until later in the day. Maybe not until after dark. She, too, was tired, and was going to have to stop and at least get something to eat.

When she had ridden away from the muddy banks of the Gila River, she had felt nearly invulnerable. So solid, so firm and strong was her determination, she thought it might carry her forever. The fire within her had burned more brightly than ever.

But she was not superhuman after all. She was exhausted and hungry. Also, she feared, a little nervous, edgy perhaps. How else to describe the feeling that someone watched her, tailed her maybe? For the hundredth time since darkness had fallen the previous evening, Blaze glanced back over her shoulder.

Nothing, no one was there. No one ever was. It was simply her imagination. It had to be. If she were in any danger, she would sense it. Her instincts were keen. Over the last several months they had been sharply honed. Nevertheless, she was grateful to reach the thriving town at last. Among other things, it looked like rain.

Two hours outside Phoenix, the full weight of exhaustion descended on Blaze. She had eaten, and brought hay and grain for Lonesome at the livery. They had rested an hour and set out again. Blaze had thought she would be fine. She couldn't have been more wrong.

Blaze could hardly keep her eyes open, and Lonesome stumbled from time to time. Worse, however, was the haunting memory that had begun to torment her. A hard, thin mouth; high, angular cheekbones. And pale blue eyes that could see into her very soul. She was riding away from him. Farther and farther away. She would probably never see him again. Why did the thought send a spear through her heart?

Blaze did not wish to probe her emotions any deeper. Her task, her journey, was difficult enough as it was. Even the weather was making everything worse.

Blaze shivered, aware the thin flannel shirt was not going to be much protection. Early spring on the desert, even the low desert, was not very warm to begin with. With the sun hidden behind low-hanging clouds, and a stiffening breeze lifting the hair from her shoulders, she was growing colder by the moment. She should stop and extract her poncho from the bedroll, she knew. But that would mean another delay, and she was anxious to catch up with Ring. If it had been raining up north for long, as it looked like, Blackjack would be swollen, and he'd need help crossing the creek.

Blaze had barely had time to ponder the grim state of affairs when lightning rent the purplish-gray skies, followed by a crash of thunder that brought Lonesome's head up sharply . . . Any moment it was going to start to rain.

But she was close now. The mountains reared up on either side of her. The valley floor rose, then leveled again. The stately desert saguaros were left behind and now boulders, mesquite, and prickly pear were her companions. Blackjack Creek was just ahead.

The first fat raindrops plopped on her nose.

Ring and Sandy had their hands full. Lightning and the ensuing roll of thunder had spooked the herd badly. They were milling and snorting, ears alternately pricked and flattened, senses alert to any danger.

"Go 'round 'em to the left," Ring shouted over another rumble of thunder. "Head off the lead mare if she tries to make a run. I'm going back to check on Rowdy."

Sandy merely nodded and took off in the direction Ring had indicated. Ring doubled back, toward the ever-swelling creek.

They'd gotten across just in time, but Rowdy's

mules had had a tough time pulling the heavily loaded wagon up the far bank. Ring wanted to make certain they'd made it safely onto high ground. He also hoped, prayed, he was going to see the most welcome sight of Blaze riding in his direction.

His first wish was granted. Rowdy and the team were coming toward him, pots and pans clanging in the back of the wagon as they bounced over rocks and ruts in the road. Thank God. Blackjack was running faster, foaming and rushing at its banks, reaching ever higher. Ring's spirits dropped into his boots.

Even if she came now, she couldn't make it across. It might be days before the creek was back to normal. He had no choice. He was going to have to leave her and go on. Ring tightened his grip on the reins, preparing to turn his mare and return to the herd. And then he saw her.

Blaze muttered an unladylike curse under her breath. The situation was clear to her the moment Blackjack came into sight.

Ring and the herd had crossed the creek. Just in time, apparently. She was too late. Lonesome snorted and tossed his head when she halted him on the southern bank.

"Go back," Ring shouted.

Blaze stubbornly shook her head. "You go on," she yelled back. "I'll camp here until I can cross. I'll catch up."

"No," Ring bellowed, his apprehension growing so rapidly it seemed to crowd out the very air in his lungs. "You don't understand. Get back . . . get away from the bank!"

She didn't understand. Not at first. Then fear took a stranglehold around her throat until she felt she couldn't draw a breath. The ground was disappearing from beneath Lonesome's hooves, crumbling away into the rising waters.

Blaze hauled hard on the reins. Lonesome responded instantly, and pivoted where he stood. His front legs came off the ground as he prepared to make a great, noble-hearted leap to safety. For naught.

The ground simply vanished. The brown bank dissolved into the churning creek. Blaze felt the sensation of sinking, felt Lonesome struggling beneath her, valiantly reaching for stable ground.

But the water dragged them. Blaze felt its wetness on her lower legs, to her knees. She felt Lonesome's hindquarters swing out as his back legs lost what little purchase they had maintained. Then the water was over her thighs, up to her waist. She clung, desperately, to Lonesome's mane as his front legs separated from the bank. They were swept to the middle of the wide, raging creek.

Blaze thought she screamed once. She wasn't sure. She became separated from her horse. The last she saw of him was his head, barely held above water, rushing away from her around a bend. Then she went under.

Everything was black. There was no sun, no light, no air in the world she had entered. She fought for the surface. With every ounce of strength, she pulled for the daylight.

Blaze bobbed up once. She opened her mouth and took a great gulp of air. Then something hit her in the back of the head. Pain blossomed like a white light behind her eyes. She swallowed muddy water.

And knew no more.

CHAPTER THIRTEEN

THE DARKNESS WAS DARKER THAN NIGHT. THERE were no dreams. There was only the endless abyss. She had no breath, no heartbeat, no rhythm of life. She floated in the void. There was simply nothing.

And then a sensation. Cold. Bone-numbing, heart-stopping cold. She was in the belly of a monster formed of ice. She had been swallowed and could not escape. She wished for death. She descended back into the void.

The cold returned. It was not painful this time, however, merely unpleasant. Blaze was aware of shivering. She shook so hard she felt she had no control whatsoever of her limbs. Her teeth clacked together painfully.

Slowly, the chill retreated. The shivering lessened. She felt the beginnings of warmth against the length of her body. She allowed herself to slip back into the dark place. This time, there was no fear.

Dreams rocked and lulled her. She lay in a meadow, fragrant and green. The scent of grass, and good, rich soil filled her nostrils. Sunshine beat upon her, and warmed her; breast, belly, thighs. She felt warm and wonderful. The dream slowly faded.

Consciousness returned. Blaze knew she was awake because of the terrible dryness of her tongue. She was unable even to lick her lips. Her eyes seemed to be glued shut.

But it was all right, she thought, to keep them closed a little longer. Because the dream was gone, but the memory of warmth remained. Her entire body felt pleasantly heated, and comforted. Memory tugged at the edges of her mind, but she thrust it aside. Everything could wait until she waited, rested, just a few more precious moments. Blaze snuggled into the warm spot just a little tighter.

And felt her flesh rub against something soft. She was immediately aware that she was entirely naked. What she lay against was deer hide, but she wasn't wearing it. She wriggled again.

There was something hard beneath the deerskin. Furthermore, she now realized there were two hard, muscular arms encircling her naked form. The heat she felt emanated from the long, lean body pressed against her own.

Panic flooded Blaze's body as effectively as both the cold and the warmth had done. The fear racing through her blood lent strength to her exhausted limbs, and she leapt to her feet in the space of a heartbeat. She found herself looking down into a pair of pale blue eyes.

It was as if the doe had come unexpectedly upon the wolf. Blaze froze, eyes wide, too terrified to run. Too frightened to decide which way to flee. She simply stared down at the man who sprawled on the ground at her feet; at the long, lean form clad in his tight, beaded buckskins; the long, shining, blue-black hair spread beneath his head like a satin pillow; the high, hard jut of his cheekbones and the bowlike curve of his upper lip.

Fear leaked from her as water from a damaged vessel. In its place came another feeling. But it was one that left her equally weak and trembling. Blaze licked her lips. What was happening to her? The question faded into insignificance when she realized the state she was in.

One hand reached to cover the evidence of her

133

womanhood. The other pulled her long hair over her shoulders to hide the swell of her breasts. A low sound issued from Bane's throat. It might have been a chuckle. Or a groan of desire. Blaze felt the fire of humiliation burn in her cheeks.

"Here. Cover yourself." Bane rose to his feet in a single, fluid motion. He handed her the colorfully woven blanket they had been lying on.

Blaze snatched it from him and quickly wrapped herself in its length. Slowly, she felt the heat drain from her face. The trembling in her knees did not abate. "Wh . . . what . . . how?" she stammered.

"Come and sit by the fire. I will tell you."

For the first time Blaze noticed she was in a small campsite. A fire crackled within a ring of stones. Her wet clothes had been spread on the branches of a sage bush to dry. Memory came back like the flood she had been washed away in, and Blaze spun around.

"My . . . my horse. Is he . . ."

"I have not found your horse."

He made the statement flatly, but Blaze thought she detected a note of sympathy in his tone. It pushed her tears even closer to the surface. Lonesome. Blaze swallowed.

"I have some quail," Bane resumed. "I haven't had time to roast them. It seemed wise to put some heat into you instead."

To her chagrin, the furious blush returned to her cheeks. Unbidden, the memory of his long, hard body pressed to hers returned. The heat drained from her face to warm the rest of her body. Then the mention of quail penetrated her consciousness. She was starving. It must have shown in her expression.

"Don't worry," he said encouragingly. "They won't take long."

Blaze saw Bane had already expertly cleaned the savory birds and skewered them on fire-hardened sticks. Moments later they were crackling over a fire. Her mouth watered uncontrollably.

"Sit." Bane had his saddle blanket laid on the ground by the fire. "And tell me how you came to be in the belly of the river."

Blaze closed her eyes and shuddered. She sank, cross-legged, onto the saddle blanket. "Stupidly," she replied simply. "I never should have ridden onto the bank. The water was too swift, the footing too dangerous."

"Too dangerous," Bane repeated. "Yes." He nodded slowly. "I heard the cowboy shout to you to go back. I would have added my voice to his, but it was too late."

Blaze stiffened as the realization washed through her. "You . . . you saw?"

"Yes. And feared I would not be able to outrun the river and pull you from its grasp."

Openmouthed, Blaze stared at the man who now sat beside her, also cross-legged. "How . . . how *did* you get ahead of me?"

Bane nodded toward the black mare tethered a short distance away. "In the Apache tongue, she is called 'Drinker of the Wind.' She came by her name for good reason."

Blaze glanced at the valiant mare gratefully, only to be sharply reminded of Lonesome. Tears welled in her eyes once again, and she looked away quickly.

"I'm grateful to you," she whispered. "More grateful than you know."

Bane remained silent. Blaze risked a glance at him from the corner of her eye. She could not help but recall her thoughts as she had ridden away from Phoenix. She had feared she would never see him again. Now he had saved her life. Something odd seemed to be happening in the pit of her stomach. And a burning question seared her tongue. She could only quench the fire by giving it voice.

"You . . . saw me at the creek bank," she said at last in a small voice. "Have you been . . . been following me?"

There it was, finally; a smile she could be certain of. The corners of his gracefully curved mouth rose ever so slightly.

"I follow only my destiny," Bane replied enigmatically.

Whatever was wrong with Blaze's stomach was getting worse. "You're headed north, then, as I am," Blaze said cautiously.

"Like you, I have discovered that the prey I hunt no longer dwells in the valley of the sun. I, too, must go where my trail leads me."

It was Blaze's turn to hold silence. She tried to remember every word Bane had said to her. It wasn't difficult. Their meetings had been few, and every moment of them had been etched into her memory. Finally, she took a deep breath.

"You've said before we have a common goal. Vengeance." When she paused, Bane nodded almost imperceptibly. Blaze continued. "Is it possible you think our shared purpose would be better served riding together?"

"Is it possible you do not know it is for this reason I have followed you?"

Blaze's breath caught in her throat. She recalled the feeling of being watched. The way he had come to her and Ring's aid with the band of Apache braves. Her arrival on the mountaintop to find him already there. A sense of unreality fell upon her like a fur-lined mantle settling about her shoulders, so soft she could barely tell it was there. She looked deeply into his light eyes.

"Why have you been watching me?" Her voice

was so low she barely heard it herself. "And how long have you followed me?"

Bane's expression was inscrutable. He took a long, slow breath into his lungs. Blaze watched his chest expand, relax.

"The path we follow," he began at length, "is a lonely one. I think I do not need to tell you this."

Blaze thought she gave a small shake of her head, but she could not be certain. She seemed transfixed by the gaze and the words of the man beside her.

"I saw you first when you rode out from the town on your horse of the Nez Perce," Bane went on. "I knew who you were at once, for rumor has swifter wings than the insect eaters that fly at night."

Bane paused and his mouth compressed into a thin, white line. Blaze could not tear her eyes from his, and her breath came rapidly through parted lips.

"You are she who buried her village," Bane murmured in a thick voice. "Who walked naked into the mountains. Who comes, like legend, back to the valley of the sun. Yes, I know you. I know your purpose is as mine. It could be no other. The only thing I do not know is the face of your enemy. But, I will aid you as long as our roads run in the same direction. And perhaps along the way I will find who *I* seek as well."

It wasn't possible. Yet it was happening. He had been watching her. He wished to join her, to help her.

"What . . . what about your . . . those braves? The ones—"

"Comrades of the moment, no more."

"But they . . . they looked to you as their leader, and they were, I mean, they might have—"

"I led no one, but rode with the brothers of my blood because I chanced upon them along my road."

"But they . . . they . . ."

"It is hard to be Indian," Bane said sternly. "We have little left to call our own. Our land disappears like carrion beneath the hunger of the vultures. Our herds have been hunted until there is nothing but their blood that soaks the ground. There is little to eat, less to do. But much, much anger."

Blaze wondered that she did not feel chastised. She felt only a deep well of sadness. "Why do you choose to share their fate," she found herself asking, "when there is white in you also?"

A tic jumped under Bane's left eye. He turned his head and spat onto the dry ground. "Do you wish my company on your journey?" he asked abruptly.

"I—" Blaze snapped her jaws shut. She clenched her teeth tightly.

Not even an old grandmother could make up such a night tale as the one Blaze found herself living. Why should she not have the company of this man of mixed blood? Other things even more fantastic had already

139

happened to her. Why shouldn't she travel in the company of someone whose heart beat to the same rhythm as her own?

And why shouldn't she dream that one day she might know the strength of those long, slender fingers on her body, and the feel of his breath on her lips?

The fire popped and crackled as fat from the roasted birds dripped into the flames. The hoarse, sharp cry of an eagle pierced the thick and murky dusk. Blaze clutched the blanket a little more tightly to her breast.

"Yes," she whispered.

The clicks and grunts and squeaks of the night filled the air with sound, although the fire had grown silent and only embers glowed. Blaze's belly was full and her river-washed clothes felt good against her skin. She sat with her knees drawn up, arms folded over them, chin on her forearms.

Stars blanketed the sky, but the moon was only a sliver. She was glad of the darkness. It was difficult not to look at him. Blaze sighed quietly, taking a deep breath and releasing it as slowly as she could.

The sense of unreality had deepened. The morning, the near-drowning in the river, seemed a hundred years ago. Ring, Sandy, and Rowdy might have been people she had merely dreamed, her entire sojourn in Phoenix a chimera. All that existed was now, this moment, sitting in the night with a light-eyed, half-breed Apache. A man whose mission was the same as her own. They were killers. They would not rest until their murders had been done.

Adding to the fantastical nature of the situation was an undeniable attraction to Bane. Bane.

Bane of the white man.

Bringer of Thunder to the Apache.

A shudder trembled through Blaze's body. She wasn't sure what it all meant yet; his name, his destiny. Her fate joined to his. The path they would travel together that was starting in darkness. She knew one thing only.

She was drawn to this course as surely and strongly as the eagle is drawn to the sky. It seemed she had known it, somewhere deep in her soul, the very first time she had seen him. She had known, in her heart, that meeting him on the mountain was no coincidence. She knew he had followed her, and she had felt him. Even as she felt him now, sitting alone in the darkness. His eyes were open, regarding the night, she knew, though she could not see. His ears took in every sound of the desert, his skin felt each nuance of the wind.

What seemed a long time later, Bane rose and unfolded the blankets he had neatly put away. He laid them on the ground, side by side, and gestured to them wordlessly.

Blaze's initial reaction was not an honest one. She shook her head and reached for the blanket to move it to the opposite side of the fire. She never got any farther than bending down.

He had pulled her from the flood, shared his warmth with her. He was her companion now, for good or evil. She ignored her foolish response and lay down at his side.

Once again he shared the heat of his body with her. She was aware of every inch of it where he pressed against her side. It was nothing compared to the heat that inexplicably churned in her belly.

The desert had grown silent by the time Blaze felt her eyelids grow heavy. Bane had not moved so much as the twitch of a single muscle. His breathing was deep and regular.

It was a blessing to slip over the threshold of sleep at last.

CHAPTER FOURTEEN

LYING ASLEEP FOR SO LONG BLAZE FELT DROWSY AND thickheaded. She pushed herself up on her elbows and looked around her sleepily.

Bane was nowhere to be seen. His blanket was folded, and she saw that he had left a piece of jerky and a canteen for her lying on top. As she chewed on the dried bison meat, she attempted to restore order to her hair. It was then she noticed his saddle blanket and saddle were gone. It didn't surprise her. She hadn't sensed his presence.

The day promised to be warm and cloudless. Blaze idly plucked at an errant tuft of grass and squinted into the bright blue sky. The sun had risen halfway to its zenith, and she began to wonder what Bane was about. She hadn't long to question before she heard the distinctive rhythm of hoofbeats. Her heart quickened to the beat.

Beyond the lightly grassed riverbank where they had passed the night was a thick, hedge-like growth of sage and mesquite. Shadowing it was a stand of cotton-wood trees. Blaze looked in their direction, ears alert to the sounds Bane must make when he approached her.

"I trust you slept as well as you slept long."

Blaze spun on her heel. Her heart threatened to jump out of her chest.

"You have eaten. Good. It is time to go."

Blaze took a moment to allow her heart and respiration to get back to normal. She retrieved the blanket she had folded.

"Put it with my bedroll, across the mare's withers. You will ride behind me."

A now-familiar sadness pricked at Blaze's eyelids. "I'll need to find a horse of my own soon. I need to catch up with Ring, let him know I'm safe, anyway. I'm sure he'll give me another."

Bane remained silent, thoughtful, for a long moment, eyes slightly narrowed. Blaze had the distinct feeling he was looking directly into her heart.

"We will find your friend," he said abruptly. "It will not be difficult."

What *was* difficult, Blaze found, was riding behind Bane. He took his foot from the stirrup so she could use it to mount. The black mare shifted nervously as

Blaze swung onto her back and automatically reached around Bane's waist to steady herself. Her heart increased its rhythm at once, and her arms, where they touched him, felt as if they burned. She snatched them away and gripped the cantle of his saddle.

Bane had merely to tighten his legs around the black mare's girth and she bounded away. Blaze was nearly unseated and forced to throw her arms around Bane's body again. Surrendering to the melting heat of it, she closed her eyes and concentrated instead on the motion of the horse.

It took only a few short moments to return to the ford. Blaze saw at once that the torrent had subsided. A shallow, narrow stream ran down the center of the riverbed, and the mare leaped it daintily. She moved back into an easy lope.

Blaze had expected Bane to ride straight along the trail. The signs of a herd of horses and a trailing wagon, heavily laden, were evident. But he turned instead and rode along the edge of the river. It was much the same as the opposite side, with brush and a scattering of cottonwoods. Thin patches of grass grew in sunlight close to the water. Bane halted.

"Your horse . . . he was valuable to you?"

Blaze hesitated. It occurred to her Bane might think her foolish if she told him what was in her heart. On the other hand, she was certain he would think less of her if she didn't tell him the truth.

"Not only was he a gift from a friend, but he . . . he was my . . . companion. I cared about him very much."

Bane made a sound that could have been a grunt. He threw his right leg forward, over the mare's withers, and slipped to the ground. "Come with me."

Puzzled, Blaze followed Bane. He moved quickly through the brush and into the shade of a trio of cottonwoods. Blaze felt a sob catch in her throat.

The horse had been grazing. He looked up when he saw the humans approach, and his ears pricked sharply. He whickered a greeting and tossed his head, then started in Blaze's direction.

"Lonesome," Blaze murmured, face pressed to his warm, sweet-smelling hide. Her arms wrapped about his neck. When she was sure her tears had dried, she turned back to Bane. "Thank you," she whispered, not trusting her voice.

"I did nothing, merely used my eyes to see him."

Blaze patted Lonesome's shoulder, and felt her saddle and bedroll to make sure all was still intact. "Still damp, but everything appears to be in order."

Without another word, Bane returned to his mare and mounted. Blaze checked her horse's girth, pulled a piece of grass from his bit, and swung into the saddle. It felt good. Smiling, she followed Bane.

The land sloped steadily uphill. Mountains reared

up on either side of them, and an occasional rockfall forced them to find new trails. Only an occasional weed or scraggly cactus clung to life in shallow crevasses in the cliff faces. Hawks wheeled overhead.

The tracks they followed were hard for Blaze to see, but Bane seemed to have no trouble whatsoever. They rode along steadily, until the sun turned into a flaming ball that hung just above the horizon. At that moment they reached a plateau, and the horses jogged for the joy of level ground beneath their feet. Before them spread a vast tableland covered in short, dry, yellow grass, dotted with boulders and small patches of stunted prickly pear. The entire land was bathed in pink. It was a sight that filled her with a kind of quiet content. Another sight filled her with joy.

A herd of horses grazed on the mesa, heads low, tails swishing. Near a cook wagon, a spiral of smoke from a cook fire curled into the sky.

Blaze glanced briefly at Bane, but his features were devoid of expression. She wanted to thank him, but knew what his reaction would be. Instead, she urged Lonesome into a canter and headed toward the grazing horses.

Ring sat atop a reasonably smooth boulder, forearms on his knees, head hanging. He ignored the enticing smells coming from Rowdy's oversized skillet. He paid no heed to Sandy, who rode slowly around the perimeter of the herd. He did not notice the concerned glances the two men exchanged when Sandy's route took him past the cook wagon. He was alone with his misery, and it was exactly where he wanted to be.

There was no denying it, not any longer. He had loved Blaze, loved her with all his heart, all his soul. She was beautiful, her beauty both wild and delicate at the same time. Merely watching her had fascinated him, she was so at ease within her skin and moved with such grace. The speed with which she had learned to ride a horse was remarkable. The passion with which she undertook to learn each new task had amazed him. To his dying day he would miss her, and he would carry regret with him to his grave. Ring sighed heavily and scrubbed the stubble on his chin with both hands.

He never did find out what had happened in her past that had set her on the course she had followed. She was hell-bent on revenge, that much he knew. But he did not know who, or why. Perhaps, if he had known, he might have been able to help her. If she had loved him in return, just a little, he might have been able to change things for her.

He could not, however, change the course of the

river that had taken her. Despite his grief, Ring wondered if it wasn't better this way after all. What would her life have been like if she had pursued her death quest? How could she, a woman alone, have tracked down and killed whoever it was she thought needed killing?

He remembered how she had told him, coolly, of killing a man for the bounty. He supposed she had it in her. The passion she applied to everything else would surely aid her in her search. But what then? What would be left of her life if she achieved vengeance? It was a lonely road she had wished to travel, and in the end there would have been nothing but more loneliness.

No. Ring shook his head. It wasn't what he wanted for her. It was no life at all. And his kind of life, the things he could have offered her, would never have been acceptable to her.

In spite of all the rationalizing, however, the depth of Ring's grief was bottomless, and from the abyss came bitter tears that spilled down his cheeks and threatened to unman him. He covered his eyes.

"Ring? Hey, Ring."

His head came up, and his gaze found Sandy.

"Ring . . . look."

He turned in the direction Sandy indicated. His jaw dropped.

It couldn't be. It wasn't possible. He had seen her

go into the river. He'd seen her in the grip of its power, saw her go under. . .

Ring didn't even care who the rider was who followed at a distance. His mind could contain only one thought as he started to run toward her. She was alive.

As soon as Blaze saw his face, she realized what he had been through, and her heart ached for him. Her only thought was to comfort the man who had been so kind to her, who had become her greatest friend.

Blaze slipped from Lonesome's back before he'd come to a full halt. It seemed the most natural thing in the world to step into the embrace Ring held wide for her. She returned the strength of his arms, and reveled for a long moment in the comforting feel of his hug, and the warmth of his friendship. When they stepped apart at last, Ring held on to her shoulders and examined her, drank in every inch of her, from head to toe.

"I thought you were dead," he said hoarsely.

Blaze gave a small, mirthless chuckle. "So did I. And I would have been, but for Bane."

Ring finally surrendered his attention to the second rider. He recognized him immediately. He recognized something else as well, and dropped his hands from Blaze's shoulders. He gave a single nod to the still-mounted man.

"I guess I owe you thanks. *All* of our thanks," Ring added pointedly, and indicated Sandy and Rowdy with a gesture. "Blaze is . . . a very good friend."

Bane remained silent, his expression unreadable. Ring turned back to Blaze.

"We looked for you. I never would have left if I thought there was a chance you could be—"

"Hush." Blaze laid a finger to his lips. "I know you never would have left if you'd thought there was any hope for me. Even *I* had given up hope. It's a miracle Bane was able to save me."

Blaze looked up at Bane, and Ring saw something in her gaze that added fresh pain to his already injured heart. He took a step away from her.

"Well, I . . . I guess the least we can do is offer you hospitality. Rowdy's been cookin' somethin' that smells real good, and there's plenty of room around the fire for two more bedrolls."

Once again Blaze looked at Bane, and Ring saw him give the faintest of nods. Ring felt mingled relief and heartache.

She was alive. He'd have a few more hours in her company. But any frail hope he had ever harbored that she might change her mind and ride on with him tore into tatters and was blown away in the night breeze that blew across the plateau. Forcing a smile to his lips, Ring turned and walked back into camp.

CHAPTER FIFTEEN

". . . AND SELL THE HERD IN WESTPORT," RING replied to one of Bane's rare questions. "By summer's end we'll be on our way west again, pickin' up more horses, then south for the winter. Start the process all over."

If Bane had a reaction to anything Ring said, Blaze couldn't tell. She watched the firelight flicker over his features, but it was only shadow and light that moved. His expression never altered.

"Yeah, start all over agin," Sandy repeated, and rubbed his hands together nervously. He cast a sidelong glance at Bane. No matter the man had saved Blaze. There was something about him that made Sandy as wary as a cat on a porch full of rockers. His silence, maybe. Or those light eyes. He looked at Rowdy, but he was calmly whittling a stick into a toothpick.

"Well." Blaze cleared her throat. "I'd like to thank you for the dinner, Rowdy. And you, Ring. Thanks for . . . everything." She left it at that.

"That sounds a lot like a good-bye to me," Ring replied. He said it lightly, although his spirit was anything but light.

Blaze shifted uncomfortably. She resisted the urge to look over at Bane. There would be no help for her there anyway.

"I've . . . I've decided to go on with Bane," she said at length. "We're headed in the same direction, and—"

Ring held up a restraining hand. "You don't have to explain, Blaze. You're a grown woman, able t'make your own decisions."

Blaze knew how hard the words were for him. She swallowed back a lump in her throat. It wasn't easy for him, she knew, to watch her ride away, much less alone with a man like Bane.

"I'll be back this way again, like as not," she added. "Don't think you're getting rid of me that easily." Blaze attempted a smile, but failed.

"Think I'll turn in," Rowdy said to no one in particular.

"Good idea," Sandy said quickly.

The other three remained motionless while Sandy and Rowdy moved from the fire to lay out their bedrolls. It was Blaze who finally gave up, the tension grating on her like sand.

"It's late for me, too," she said, and left the circle of light. She was grateful for the cool darkness, and spread out her blankets without further ado.

It wasn't long before she heard the sounds of the other two men preparing for the night. Neither said a word to the other. Blaze turned over and buried her face in her blanket, musty smelling from the river. It was a long time before she slept.

Dawn came swiftly to the high plateau. The night breeze had stiffened, and the horses stamped and snorted, eager to be off. Having said her good-byes to Sandy and Rowdy, she watched them move off with the herd. Now came the most difficult moment of all.

Ring sat astride his favorite bay mare. Blaze remembered the first time she had seen Duchess. And Sandy and Ring.

She maneuvered Lonesome alongside Ring's horse. She didn't want to look at him, face the sadness she knew she would see there. But she owed it to him. It was her turn to bear a part of the burden, a portion of the pain.

"There are things I have to thank you for that I can't even put a name to," Blaze began quietly. "You've helped me in so many ways, Ring. Given me so much."

"Not one ounce more than you gave me," Ring replied soberly. Then the corners of his mouth lifted into the semblance of a smile. "'Cept one thing. And I believe mebbe you should be a bit beholdin' for it."

Blaze's brow arched. "Anything," she said quickly. "Tell me what it is. I'd do anything to repay you, Ring."

He touched a finger to his temple and traced a streak of lightning. "Your name. It's a pretty fine and fancy name I gave you there, in the mountains. Think mebbe I'd like to have some compensation."

She heard the levity in his tone and tried to return his smile. "Name your price, Ring Crossman."

He held his smile for a moment longer. It slipped away without will or conscious thought. "When you get through this, Blaze," he said softly. "When you get to the other side of whatever it is, I'd like to know your real name. Where you come from. How it all began."

It hurt. Something within her hurt so badly she wasn't sure she could withstand the pain. She looked down at her hands holding the reins. After a long, hard moment, she was able to nod.

"When I get through it," she whispered. Blaze lifted her chin and looked straight into Ring's steady gaze. She disregarded the tears that streamed down her cheeks. "When I get through it," she repeated, "you've got yourself a deal."

"I'll look forward to that, then." Ring lifted a hand in a kind of salute, and nodded briefly in Bane's direction. He wheeled his mare and galloped off after the retreating herd.

Silence closed around them. Tiny white butterflies flitted among even smaller wildflowers hidden in the grass. The breeze smelled faintly of horse dung and dry earth, and the distant, pungent perfume of mountain pines. With nimble fingers, Blaze swiftly plaited her hair into a single braid.

"I guess it's time to ride."

Bane regarded Blaze without reply. Then he turned, squinted slightly, and studied the horizons.

"The herd will go north and east," he said at last. "That is the best route over the mountains to the cowboy's destination. We will go straight to the north."

The black mare danced, sensing her rider's readiness to set out. Lonesome stood patiently, as always. Blaze picked up her reins to signal her own readiness, but still Bane made no move. He continued to gaze into the distance. After awhile, Blaze realized the herd was almost out of sight.

Bane looked over at her, and Blaze thought she

saw a subtle softening of his features. To her surprise, he reached over and gently wiped the tears from her cheeks. He straightened again in his saddle.

"Now, it is time to ride." He set off at once at a lope.

CHAPTER SIXTEEN

By DAY'S END THEY HAD REACHED THE PONDEROSA-
pine-clad slopes of the northern Arizona mountains.
Shadows were deep beneath the towering trees, and
the sound of their horses' hooves was muffled by the
thick carpet of fallen needles on the forest floor. Startled squirrels raced up tree trunks, tails twitching. A
jay scolded them for their trespass and, as the moon
rose, they heard the howl of a wolf, and the answer of
his mate.

Blaze wondered if Bane had plans to stop for the
night. They had halted only once during the long day,
to water the horses at a thin stream. They had chewed
on some of the dried meat he kept in his pack to keep
themselves going, but Blaze wasn't sure how much
longer she was going to last. It never occurred to her
to ask. She neither wished to disturb the comfortable

silence between them, nor appear to question Bane in any way. Her trust in him was implicit. It disturbed her only a little, and only because she thought it probably should. She had, after all, entrusted her life to, and joined her destiny with, a near-total stranger.

It didn't matter. He had saved her life, and more than once probably. He had lain with her to give her life and warmth, not take her honor. He had provided for her, guided her, had even comforted her in his way. Still, none of those things mattered, Blaze realized. She would have trusted him anyway. There was simply something within the man, something at his core, that she connected with. And it had nothing to do with the blood quests they shared.

The howling of wolves had become the chorus of the night. An owl swooped suddenly from the branches of a pine and disappeared into the darkness to the eerie, whistling flap of wings. The moon was a bright silver crescent amid its attendant stars. Blaze's eyelids fluttered closed.

She awoke to find herself slipping from the saddle into Bane's arms. He set her gently on her feet, and looked into her eyes to make sure she was awake. Then he released her and walked away. To her puzzlement, he began to dig in the soft earth with the wicked-looking blade of the knife he wore at his waist. She noticed, once her senses had fully returned, that he worked at the base of a pine that bore a subtle slash mark.

In a few minutes, Bane pulled a large, irregular bundle from the trench he had dug in the earth. It appeared to be buffalo hide. He unwrapped it and spread the contents before him. Blaze was amazed.

There was more jerky; "Venison, buffalo," Bane informed her. There was also pemmican and an assortment of dried berries, ammunition, three canteens of water, and a change of clothes, beaded deerskin similar to what Bane wore now. He sat back on his haunches and gestured.

"Eat," he said simply. "It is far to the next banquet I have laid by."

Blaze knelt at his side, an incredulous smile trying to form on her lips. Bane looked down on her, and although his lips did not curve into a response, she thought she saw a twinkle in his eye. It might have only been a sliver of moon glow, but it sent a happy warmth through her nonetheless.

The night grew cold on the mountain, and Bane had laid no fire. Blaze took a second flannel shirt from her pack and started to put it on.

"This buffalo surrendered his life to keep me from starving. And to keep you from freezing." Bane removed all the items from the hide and laid it out, hair side up, directly under the ponderosa. "Sit, and be warmed."

Blaze did as she had been bidden. She gratefully

accepted the blanket he put around her shoulders. He sat across from her and went to work honing his knife on a whetstone. She listened to the rasping sound of it for several long minutes.

"Bane?"

He looked up for the fraction of a second, spat on the stone to aid his task, and returned to it. In the thin moonlight, the crown of his head shone blue-black.

"Who was Apache, Bane?" Blaze persisted. "Your mother?"

He looked up again. "Does it matter?"

"Not at all."

He retuned to his chore. "My mother," he replied shortly.

"Was she beautiful?"

"Yes."

"She raised you, didn't she?"

"My clan, my village, raised me, as it is with all Indian children."

"But, I mean, you lived with her?"

"We shared a tipi, yes."

Silence fell again. Some kind of small animal chattered nearby. Bane put away his stone, cleaned his blade, and sheathed it. He came to where she sat on the buffalo hide, and hunkered down before her.

"I understand what you wish to know," he said. "So, I will tell you."

"Bane, you don't have—"

"No, it's right that you know. I have knowledge of what was done to your people. I understand why you seek the blood of the murderers. You should know why I seek the blood of my father."

It felt as if a chill hand had been laid upon her heart. Blaze shivered and pulled the blanket closed at her throat.

"Your . . . your father?"

"The one who put the seed in my mother's womb. Yes." The tic jumped under his eye. "The white man who took what was not his. The abomination who raped and savaged the woman who was pledged to another, then left her for dead. The one who stole her future, her mind, her life, and left her only with a quickened belly. Yes. My father."

Blaze was too stunned to speak. She looked into Bane's eyes and was suddenly, strangely, and horribly reminded of the man who had taken the lives of so many of her people, and who had murdered her brother. Memory and loss were like talons closing about her chest. She felt as if she couldn't breathe, and the pain was nearly unendurable. Blaze reached out and grasped Bane's hands.

"They will die," she whispered hoarsely. "All of them. The butchers of my village. The man who hanged my brother. Your father. All of them."

Bane let her hold his hands. Then, slowly, his fingers curled around hers. They held on to each other thus for a long, long time.

Sometime during the night Blaze awakened without knowing why. The night had grown quiet. All she could hear was the soft sound of Bane breathing as he slept beside her. She was warm atop the hide, two blankets covering them both, the heat of the man at her side seeming to infuse her entire body.

It was unreal, all that had happened, the many twists of fate that had brought her to this moment. Bane himself. Blaze felt as if she needed to anchor herself, reach out and touch something solid to know that she dwelt in the world of reality, and not within a dream. She stretched a hand outside the blankets.

The pine needles felt cool and slightly damp from the rich, shaded earth upon which they lay. She moved her fingers and encountered a pinecone. Real things, the life of the forest. Not a dream.

An owl hooted, and Blaze felt relieved. She rolled on her side, the better to gaze on Bane's profile.

It was easy to see his Indian heritage. In profile his features were sharp and well defined. She longed to reach out and touch his shining hair, but was afraid to wake him.

In the end, she laid her head, ever so gently, on his shoulder, and rested her fingers on his chest. He stirred slightly, but Blaze did not think she had awakened him. Then she felt the weight and warmth of his hand cover hers.

She slept almost at once.

CHAPTER SEVENTEEN

BLAZE DIDN'T THINK SHE HAD EVER FELT SO SELF-conscious or out of place. The town was nothing to boast of, so why did the people seem to think so highly of themselves . . . and look down their noses at the newcomers? *Or is there something really wrong with me?* Blaze wondered miserably. She glanced over at Bane, but he appeared not to notice. He stared straight ahead and guided his mare down the center of the street.

"Bane," she hissed in an undertone, leaning from her saddle in his direction. "Is there something wrong with—?"

"No," he replied sharply, with a shake of his head. His eyes remained to the front. "There is nothing wrong with either of us. Except that you are Mexican. And I am a half breed."

"Oh." Blaze thought about what Bane had said,

and realized the awful truth of it immediately.

In Phoenix she had been accepted because of Ring. Everyone knew him, and had known his mother. Because he was one of them, they accepted who he himself accepted. She had never even thought about it.

But Bane was right. They were non-white in a white man's world. Funny, she hadn't thought of it before. But neither had she thought about Bane being Apache. The Apache were traditional enemies of her people. But Bane was not her enemy. She had not judged him by his race, but by his qualities as a man. Why did whites not judge others the same way?

"Is there anything you need?" Bane asked suddenly.

Blaze noticed they were passing a general store. She gave it some thought for a moment, then shook her head. She had everything she needed. A comb, a bar of soap, and three changes of clothes since Bane had given her the buckskins he had hidden in the Arizona mountains with the stores. She smiled at the memory.

Following that first night on the mountain, she had awakened to find herself completely wound in Bane's embrace. She had wished she might remain that way forever, and closed her eyes. She tried to remain very still so she would not wake him, and could lie there inhaling the intoxicating male scent of him for as long as possible.

But Bane was as alert to the coming of the sun as

a shift in the wind. As the sky had lightened, his eyes opened and he almost seemed to sniff the air. Blaze feigned sleep and, with sinking heart, felt him disentangle himself from her arms, rise, and stride off into the trees.

By the time he returned, Blaze managed to bring some order to her hair and had scrubbed her hands and face and teeth using a bit of water from one of the canteens. She shivered, however, in the crisp morning air. Bane noticed.

"Here. Wear these. They are more suitable on the trail we take."

He had handed her the buckskins. She ducked behind a tree to put them on. The first real smile she had ever seen on Bane's face appeared when she stepped back into his sight.

"What's so funny?" she had demanded, hands on the swell of her hips.

Bane simply shook his head, drew his knife, and knelt in front of her.

Bane was at least six inches taller than Blaze. The legs of the breeches extended a good six inches beyond her feet. He cut them to the right length, then turned his attention to the sleeves. They, too, hung below her hands several inches. Blaze had a fair idea how silly she looked, and a giggle erupted from her throat.

Bane straightened and looked directly into her

eyes. "Indeed, you are a sight to make a man smile."

He had said it with all seriousness, no trace of humor. Blaze felt the smile slip from her lips as her heart hammered a new rhythm.

Bane had been correct. The deerskin was warmer and more comfortable than her store-bought clothes. Neither was she too hot when the sun rose to midday, as she had feared. Even better, she like the fact that she looked like she belonged with Bane.

They had spent three days and three nights going through Arizona. On the fourth morning he had led her into a land beyond wonder, beyond imagination.

The mountains, pine trees, grassy slopes, and cool nights were behind them. Once again they were in desert-like country. But not any desert she had even dreamed could exist.

The valley floor was dotted with strange and fantastical rock formations. Some resembled mutated mushrooms. Others were like church spires pointing into the sky. Mesas rose and stretched into the distance, their sides striated with the colors of the rainbow. Blaze was in awe.

All day they had ridden through the wonderland. They saw few whites, and fewer Indians. The ones they did see, Bane informed her, belonged to the Ute tribe. The only animals they saw were distant herds of antelope and a few rabbits.

That night when they camped, Bane made a fire and roasted two fat rabbits he had shot. The buffalo hide had been left on the mountain with the remainder of the stores, but they had their blankets. They lay side by side, as usual, companions under the moon as well as the sun. But it felt different somehow. Blaze turned on her side and did something she had never done before when Bane was awake. Lightly, she placed her hand on his chest. He did not react by so much as the twitch of a single muscle.

"Bane, where are we headed? Exactly, I mean."

"We have no destination. We are hunters."

"But . . . how do we know where to search for our prey?"

Unless she had placed her hand on his chest, Blaze would never have known of Bane's sigh.

"I do not know," he admitted at length. "I know only as you do . . . that the animal I hunt is no longer in the southern deserts. He must have gone north, so we do also."

Blaze thought for a moment. Then: "'North' covers a big area."

There was a half moon in the sky. Although they lay beneath the thick-leafed branches of a gnarly scrub oak, there was enough light to see by. Blaze saw the corners of his mouth move upward ever so slightly.

"Yes. 'North' is a very big area," Bane agreed.

"So, you must have a plan. I know you." Blaze instantly regretted her words. Though the two lay side by side in the dark, it seemed too familiar a thing to say to a man like Bane. He did not, however, react as she had feared.

"You are observant for one born without Indian blood. Yes, I have a plan."

"Would you share it?"

"Why not, when we share all else?" To Blaze's surprise, Bane turned on his side, facing her. He supported himself on one arm, a hand under one cheek. His face was mere inches from her own.

"In the summer," he continued, "the Sioux nations meet at a place called Fort Laramie. They trade goods. And rumor. My . . . 'father' . . . has long preyed on my brothers, in one way or another. It is likely they will have word of him. It is likely also they will know of the butchers who take Mexican scalps, and call them Indian, to sell to the government."

An idea formed in Blaze's mind; a small spark of knowing fed the dry tinder of further knowledge. Its flame brightened a dark corner of her mind.

"Fort Laramie," she repeated, almost dreamily. "That's in the central plains, isn't it?"

Bane nodded slowly.

"It's to the north. And west."

Bane remained still.

171

"Did you . . . did you bring me this way to avoid traveling with Ring? Or to show me this amazing place?"

"I fear no man. I give you the only gift I have within my power to give."

Blaze's heart seemed to twist over and around itself inside her chest. She didn't know what to say. Then realized there was only one thing to say.

"Thank you," Blaze whispered.

Blaze sighed and hugged the memory tightly to her heart. It would sustain her during times like these.

The town, crouched at the foot of the great mountain range they had to cross, was little more than a few storefronts on a main street. Blaze looked back at the general store as they passed.

There really were a couple of things she would have liked to have. A bit of candy, for instance. She had, unfortunately, discovered she had a sweet tooth during her time with Ring.

But she and Bane had scarcely enough money left between them to buy a sack of flour, much less indulge in sweets. Which made her wonder why he had tied his mare to the hitching post in front of the local saloon.

"Bane?"

"I want information only. Wait for me."

He disappeared inside the swinging doors. It took two seconds for Blaze to decide waiting was a bad idea.

Only the bartender and an old man inhabited the bar at this time of day. They gazed at Bane curiously when he entered. Then the saloon keeper's brow lowered and his eyes narrowed.

"We ain't got nothin' you want, Injun," he growled.

"That's right. You don't. Unless you've seen a certain stranger lately."

"I seen nothin'. Get out."

Blaze had watched over the top of the doors. She pushed inside.

"What's she?" the bartender gestured with his chin. "Another half breed?"

It happened so fast Blaze was barely aware of doing it. One moment her hands were hanging loosely at her sides; the next they held pistols that were pointed at the bartender's head.

The old man uttered a short, sharp sound that might have been a laugh. The saloon keeper slowly raised his hands.

"Whoa, now," he said in an unsteady voice. "I know about them Injun tempers. Take it easy. Just take it easy."

"Yet you apparently know nothing of Mexican tempers, do you?" Blaze responded heatedly.

"It's all right," Bane said calmly. "Put your guns away."

Blaze reluctantly lowered the guns to her sides, but did not holster them. Bane turned back to the bartender.

"Strangers," he repeated. "We only want to talk about strangers."

"We . . . we get lots of strangers in here," the bartender said grudgingly. "You'll have to do better'n that."

The bartender's eyes shifted nervously from Bane to Blaze and back again. Blaze realized, in a flash, that in all their conversations, she had not once given Bane a description of the man who had murdered her brother. She would have to wait her turn, then question the saloon keeper herself.

"A big man," Bane continued, and Blaze heard the tension in his voice. "Ugly. He has a scar, here." He drew a crooked line down across his eye with one finger. "Like lightning. Like the mark in the woman's hair."

The guns dropped from her nerveless fingers and clattered on the floor.

CHAPTER EIGHTEEN

THE GREED FOR WESTERN LAND AND GOLD HAD opened many new trails. One of the most useful was the road over the great Rocky Mountain range. Though impassable in winter, late spring was a beautiful time of the year to climb to the pass. Where grass grew, on the flat ground and among the colossal upthrusts of rock, it was as green as the eye could stand. Wildflowers, purple, pink, blue, red, yellow, and white, dotted the green. Orange and golden butterflies were living blossoms floating on the mild spring breeze. Almost magically, however, snow still lay in patches in the cool shadows of the towering rock. In its own way, it was as great a wonderland to Blaze as the painted desert had been.

Though the way was scenic, it was also steep. They had stopped to rest the horses often and, once, took the time to dismount and reinforce themselves with the dried meat that had become their standard fare. Blaze had been acutely aware of Bane watching her, but she had studiously avoided his gaze. It was enough, for now, that he knew they sought one and the same man. She would give him the details later. Later, when the shock of the discovery had been absorbed into her system, and she could speak of it without the humiliation of tears and trembling.

The shadows were long and the wind cold when Bane, without a word, led them off the main trail. They climbed a grassy path that wound through the rock, until they came to a flat and verdant spot hidden by the arms of the mountain, sheltered by a trio of stunted trees. The remains of an old campfire were evident, within a circle of stones.

Blaze was not surprised. It was obvious Bane had traveled this way before, no doubt many times. She was merely grateful for his trail sense and far-seeing accommodation for future trips.

Their first priority, as always, was to care for the horses. They stripped them of their tack, rubbed them down and watered them, and, finally, hobbled them so they might graze at will. Bane started a fire, and Blaze sat as close as she could. It was early night on the mountain, as the sun sank below the level of the peaks.

The darkness deepened and Blaze continued to sit

silently. She declined food when Bane offered, and noticed he himself did not choose to eat. She knew he was giving her time, would give her all night if need be, to pull herself together and tell her tale. And she tried. But each time she attempted to form the words, to relive that horrible day, it felt as if icy fingers closed around her throat while her heart threatened to burst with grief.

It was Bane, finally, who broke the long and terrible silence. He cleared his throat, then: "The man who caused my mother to give me life was evil."

Blaze cringed at the sorrow she heard in his tone.

"But, though he stole her mind," Bane continued, "he did not also take her heart. She loved me. Her love nurtured me. I was shaped by her hand, and the hands of my people . . . not by the evil seed of my father. Please do not hate me, Blaze. I had no more choice of sire than a foal in the pasture."

Blaze opened her mouth, but no words would come. She was horrified by what Bane had said, what he apparently believed to be true and the reason for her reticence to speak.

"Bane . . . oh, Bane, no," she managed at last. She uncurled from her position on the opposite side of the fire and hurried to his side, where she knelt. A great wave of emotion welled up in her, and before she realized fully what she was doing, took his face in her hands.

Bane pulled away and took her hands from his face. He shook his head as if to deny his sadness and vulnerability to her opinion of him. Blaze grasped his shoulders instead.

"Bane, I would never think that . . . *could* never think that. I saw him, your father. I saw what he can do. You're not him."

"You saw him." Bane's voice was barely a whisper.

Blaze pressed her lips tightly together. She had to tell him. Everything. Now. She hung her head for a moment, then sat down in front of Bane.

The memories settled and collected on her like dust. She was back in the high desert, breathtaking in its spring finery. Her burro, laden with sticks, followed along behind her, tail swishing . . .

It was long into the night by the time Blaze drew to the close of her tale. It was a wonder to her that she had not broken down with the horror of reliving the experience. Bane had given her his rapt attention.

"Then I . . . I cut my brother down," Blaze said finally. "At the last. I laid him with my mother and father. And I covered the grave. Covered all of them."

Stillness settled once again. Blaze thought she could hear the sound of Bane breathing.

"He killed your family." Bane's voice was still hoarse. "He brought this upon you."

"Yes. And the others. The ones with him."

"Yet, you do not seek them?"

Blaze recalled the man at the ford on the Gila. "I learned that the man who led them died of a fever. Most of his band went west. Only the . . . scarred man . . . did not follow the gold trail."

"The scarred man," Bane repeated, as if to himself. He moved a little closer to Blaze and tilted her chin up to the firelight, as if to see her better. He traced the white in her hair with a fingertip. "Blaze," he breathed. "Blaze of lightning. It is an omen. He will be delivered to hell by you, Blaze of Lightning. And I will bring the thunder."

CHAPTER NINETEEN

NEAR THE TOP OF THE MOUNTAIN RANGE, JUST WEST of the pass, they met their first wagon train of settlers. Blaze was taken aback at first by the sheer size and noise of the procession that seemed to pass endlessly.

"Come," Bane ordered under his breath. "Stay well off the trail."

Blaze did not hesitate to obey. Even Lonesome was shy of the great, swaying wagons, the teams of horses, oxen, and mules. What struck Blaze the most, however, were the lines of weariness etched into the faces of all who passed. Even the children were subdued and quiet. There was little conversation Blaze could observe, merely exhausted men and women sitting side by side on the benches of the high wagons, swaying from side to side. Besides the noise the wagons themselves made, only the crack of whips could be heard, or the occasional shout of a driver.

More than the people, Blaze pitied the animals. The people, at least, had chosen to take the hard road west. The animals had not. Most were gaunt. Many were lame. Some had open, running sores where their harnesses bit into them and rubbed. As if to underscore her silent thoughts, the nearside wheeler of a team of mules suddenly stumbled to its knees. It struggled to get up, but seemed unable. The driver snarled, and the lash of his whip snaked toward the stricken animal. It was more than Blaze could stomach.

"Stop," she cried. "What's wrong with you?"

"Blaze," Bane hissed. "Leave it."

She seemed not to hear him. She jumped off her horse and ran to the mule, still on its knees.

"Get away from that animal, squaw," the driver bellowed. Once again he raised his whip.

Blaze ignored him, and put gentle hands on the mule's trembling withers. The lash whistled toward them both. It was Blaze, however, who was the target this time.

The pain was horrible, worse than anything she had ever imagined. A high, thin sound came to her ears, and she didn't even realize it was her own cry of agony.

The scream went through Bane like an arrow through his heart. And, in that single instant, a realization ran though his mind.

Blaze saw the driver's arm rise again. Her hands were already on their way to her holster. But someone else was faster.

Before the driver could bring down his arm and snap his wrist, an object hurled through the air. It pierced the handle of his lash and pinned it to the wagon frame. With a curse, he tried to wrench it free. The blade held fast. Blaze smiled grimly as her hands rested lightly on her pistol grips, guns still holstered. Bane had already unsheathed his rifle and held it pointed at the driver's heart.

"We don't want any trouble," Bane said, his voice low and taut with menace. "Just leave the woman alone."

The driver looked about wildly, as if searching for help. But the wagons ahead had all moved on, oblivious to the drama in their wake. Those behind were equally blind to what had transpired. The woman at the driver's side, eyes wide with fear, laid a hand on his arm. The man sat stock-still.

"Don't move a muscle. I'm just going to retrieve my knife." Holding the rifle level, Bane urged the black mare forward. She sidled up to the wagon, and he grabbed the hilt of the weapon. It came free in his hand and he sheathed it. "Blaze, go on. I'll be right behind you."

Blaze gave a low whistle, and Lonesome jogged to her side. A moment later she was riding back up the trail. She heard Bane follow. When he reached her side, they kicked their horses into a lope by mute agreement, and soon passed the last wagon in the train.

Blaze tried not to show it, but each step Lonesome took brought fresh agony to the raw weal on her back. She was wondering how much longer she could go on, when the ground leveled out and they found themselves atop the majestic mountain pass.

Pain, for a moment, was suspended, and Blaze sucked in her breath. Pine, fir, and blue spruce dotted the lawnlike grassy field. A glass-smooth lake reflected cottony clouds sailing in a bright blue sky, and the jagged peaks of distant mountains higher than the ground on which they stood.

"Bane, it's . . . beautiful," she breathed.

"Yes," Bane replied in a curiously quiet voice.

Blaze stared into Bane's light eyes and wondered what was wrong. His tone sounded odd Then it occurred to her how very little she knew about this man; the man at whose side she slept every night, but for warmth, not love, yet whose nearness heated her blood as no man had ever done . . . whose every word, every gesture, carved a memory into her heart, but whose heart was closed to her in return. He had shared his story with her, and they shared the same trail of vengeance. But what did she really know of Bane, besides his desire to avenge his mother? Her tongue, it seemed, had cleaved to the roof of her mouth. The rhythm of her heart was frantic.

"Come and sit by the lake with me," Bane said quietly. "I will wash your wound."

His gentleness was a stark contrast to the murderous intent that simmered in his soul. Which part was the real Bane? And how was he any different from she herself? Blaze shook her head and, on horseback, followed Bane to the opposite side of the mirrorlike water. Beneath a thick stand of evergreen, he dismounted and helped Blaze to the ground.

"Go, sit. I will take care of your horse."

Blaze did as she was bidden and sat, gingerly, at the water's edge. In minutes, Bane joined her.

"Lift your arms," he ordered gently. "I do not wish to have to cut this fine deerskin shirt from your back."

A joke? Had he actually made a joke? What was happening? Obediently, Blaze raised her arms. So familiar had they become with one another, she did not even consider her nakedness.

Then Bane's hands were pulling the shirt upward, slowly, taking the greatest care. The soft, well-cured hide slid smoothly over her skin and, suddenly, it was a sensual sensation almost beyond endurance. And her awareness of her nakedness abruptly became acute. Blaze had to bite her lip to keep from panting and giving away the forbidden feelings she harbored for Bane.

He must never know. It was enough to be near him.

Bane laid the shirt aside and examined the wound. Tenderly, he pressed the flesh around the weal. "It will heal quickly," he pronounced. "But it will cause you pain until it does."

"I . . . I don't mind," Blaze mumbled.

"Cold water will numb it." Bane opened Blaze's bedroll and took out one of her flannel shirts. He soaked it in the lake, then returned to sit behind her. She had, he noticed, crossed her arms across her breasts.

Blaze gasped when the icy flannel was first applied to her back. In minutes, however, the pain was significantly reduced.

"Is it better?"

Blaze could only nod.

"I'll bring you another of your shirts. It will be softer, I think, than the deerskin. No matter how fine a shirt it is."

Blaze turned just in time to see him smile. She felt as if she were melting. Arms still crossed over her breasts, she smiled tentatively, and watched Bane as he retrieved another shirt. He held it out to her.

Blaze hesitated, inexplicably shy. Why? Hadn't he undressed her, seen her unclothed form, when he had pulled her from the river? Hadn't he lain next to her, pressed to her naked flesh? Blaze took a deep breath and forced herself to uncross her arms and reach for the shirt.

It was Bane's turn to catch his breath, and he wondered at his reaction. He had seen her before, every inch of her lovely form. So, why now was there a stirring in his loins, a fire in his blood? Self-consciously, he averted his gaze as she slipped quickly into the shirt. He turned around in time to see her buttoning the last button. This time, he had to wonder at his flush of disappointment. Then he remembered the pain he had felt when the lash had kissed her back, almost as if it had wrapped itself around his shoulders instead of hers. He recalled, too, the anxiety he had felt when he had raced his mare along the riverbank, unsure whether or not he would be able to rescue Blaze from the floodwaters. Why?

Because they shared a common goal, Bane told himself quickly. And firmly. A goal more common than they ever might have dreamed. That, perhaps, was the reason he felt so intensely protective of Blaze. She *was* the vessel that would deliver his father to hell.

The rationalization did not, however, account for the uncomfortable tightness at the groin of his breeches, or the heat that rose upward into his breast. Frustration welled in Bane and finally spilled over.

"I . . . I must see about fresh meat for our dinner."

Blaze gaped as Bane spun abruptly on his heel and disappeared into the trees. To her surprise, and the gratification of her stomach, Bane returned later with a bag full of doves.

"I'll help you clean them," Blaze offered.

"There is only one knife," he replied curtly.

Blaze winced, as if stung. "All right, I'll . . . I'll cook them, then."

"If it pleases you."

The evening was a somber one. Blaze was hurt and confused by Bane's behavior. What had she done? She ran through her memory of the day's events, and experienced a horrible sinking feeling in the pit of her stomach.

When she had reached for her shirt and bared herself to him . . . had she breached the unspoken rules of their intimacy as companions? Had she unwittingly crossed some boundary he preferred remain intact? Blaze shivered.

That had to be it. The way she felt about him, she must have given him some unconscious sexual signal. But he did not feel that way about her, and therefore responded in the way he was acting now. Blaze felt sick.

In no way had he ever indicated he was interested in being more than just a friend to her. She felt as if she had just betrayed that friendship.

As a near-full moon rose above the mountains, Blaze sadly picked up her blankets and spread them beneath a fir. Some time later, she heard Bane moving about. She waited, but he never came to lie next to her.

Silently, she cried herself to sleep.

At least Blaze thought she had kept the sounds of her sadness to herself.

"Blaze?"

She froze in mid-sniffle. The sound of his voice was so close he had to be kneeling next to her.

"What is it, Blaze? Does the wound pain you?"

She had been a small child when she had last cried over a skinned knee. It galled Blaze to have to tell the lie, but what choice did she have? "Yes . . . yes, I'm . . . sorry. I didn't mean to wake you."

"I was not sleeping. Would you like me to numb the pain again?"

"That's not . . . not necessary."

"It is necessary if it causes you such distress you shed tears."

"Oh . . . *damn.*"

"Blaze—"

Blaze sat up abruptly and saw Bane was, indeed, kneeling at her side. By the light of the full moon, she saw genuine concern in his gaze. She couldn't lie to him anymore.

"My back is fine, Bane. Well, not *fine*. But it's not why . . . I mean . . ."

Blaze's long, black hair streamed over her shoulders and down her back. Highlighted by the moon, it looked like a cascade of dark water. He wanted to reach out and stroke it.

"Yes?" he prompted. "You mean . . ."

"I mean I'm . . . I'm not crying because I . . . hurt."

There were gold flecks in her dark eyes. Had he ever noticed before? "Then why do you cry?"

"Because I . . . I . . ." To her horror, tears threatened her again. The lump in her throat was huge and nearly as painful as the weal on her back. It rendered her completely unable to speak, and Blaze realized it was probably a very good thing. Had she been able to find her voice, she might have revealed her hidden heart to Bane, and driven him away forever.

Bane waited, patiently, but Blaze's only response was a renewed fountain of tears. He didn't understand, not at all. He wished to comfort the woman who had become his companion, and with whom he shared so much. He wanted to protect her, stop her pain. But all he could think to do was utter the words a village grandmother had once said to him when he was a very small boy:

"Tell me where it hurts, Blaze. Tell me where it hurts and I will make it go away."

189

He was too close. She could smell his breath, faintly herbal and woody, and it was warm against her cheek. The hair that cloaked his shoulders was black as a raven's wing. His dark eyes glittered with light like moonlight on a deep, deep lake. The planes of his face were angular, rugged, and Blaze found her fingers reaching to touch him even before she was aware of what she was doing. Just in time, before it could betray her, she snatched her hand away. But its treason was beyond her control.

Blaze's fingers brushed her lips. "Here," she whispered, not recognizing the sound of her own voice. "It hurts here."

The simplicity of the gesture, its utter sensuality and invitation, stunned Bane. He tried to think, but rational thought eluded him. He knew, on some other, deeper level, that he must not do what he was about to, but found he had no control of his body.

Blaze did not realize she had been holding her breath until Bane reached out and took her face gently in his hands. With his thumbs he stroked the ridges of her cheekbones, her temples, smoothed her furrowed brow, and, finally, traced the generous curve of her mouth with a forefinger.

She could not believe it was happening. His touch was so tender, so gentle. Did he care? Care for a woman, and not simply a companion of the trail?

Once again her traitorous body had its way, and more humiliating tears spilled from her eyes.

Bane knew he must stop, but he couldn't. He needed to say something, but was unable to even reason what it was, much less find the words to articulate it. He withdrew his hands from Blaze's face and stared at them, and thought about the power that was in them. They had taken life, and they had saved life. They had been used both for violence, and for healing. What other power might he find in them now? Could they say to her the thing that he himself did not understand?

Two tears tracked a path from Blaze's eyes to the corners of her mouth. He touched them, lightly, with his thumbs, and drew them away from her face. His fingers moved to her luxuriant hair, and he pushed it away from her face, one hand tangled in black, the other in white. Then he kissed away the path the tears had left.

The taste was sweet wine to him. Hands still bound in her hair, Bane pulled her head back so he might kiss her neck, her throat. He knew it was wrong, knew he must stop. But Blaze moaned, and the sound caused a sensual stab of pleasure that went straight to his loins. He felt her arms go about his neck, and he covered her mouth with his.

Blaze was drowning. This time, however, she was

not cold, but warm, and she did not struggle for the surface. She wanted to remain in the place where there was no light, no air, only her lover, her love. She wanted to breathe in nothing but him, his scent, his essence. She wanted only to join with him, as her heart and mind were already joined. She wished for their bodies to have one purpose, as their lives had only one.

They were naked with no memory of undressing one another. They were frenzied to be close, closer. Their mouths devoured each other. Bane lay back and pulled Blaze on top of him. Her hair fell about him like a dark curtain.

Despite the cool mountain air, their bodies were slick with sweat. Panting for breath, Blaze kissed his smooth, broad chest, and traced his nipples with the tip of her tongue. She felt the man part of him pressing hard against her abdomen, and fresh whorls and eddies of pleasure flowed through her body. She pushed herself farther down, and pressed her lips to the object of her desire. He throbbed, and the musky male scent of him suffused her with desire so intense it was almost unbearable.

Blaze pulled herself back up and kissed Bane once again. Hunger and need drove her hips into his. But he did not cooperate. Holding her tenderly away, he turned her over onto her side, then her back. Despite the pain, she would not deny him, however. Could not.

"Bane—"

"Sssshhhh." He heard her need for him in the tone of her voice. It inflamed him. But he did not ever want her to forget this time, this moment.

Blaze had not thought she could experience sensation any more keenly than she already had, pressed to her lover's body, held in his embrace. She was wrong. When he nuzzled her breast, sucked it between his teeth, and gently tugged, she feared she might swoon. First one breast, then the other, until she cried out. He had only just begun.

Bane lay against her side, propped on one elbow. With his free hand, he lightly traced the outline of her form. His fingers ran from the hollow of her throat down between her breasts, then back up again to circle each one. His touch was featherlight, and he watched with satisfaction as small bumps were raised on her flesh. Blaze groaned and her back arched.

It was almost more than Bane could bear himself. But he forced himself to remain at her side, and his fingers continued their journey, down to her belly this time, to the moist and secret treasure of her womanhood.

The sensation was beyond imagination. Blaze arched and writhed, passion ignited past all boundaries, all restraints. Her fingernails bit into the flesh of Bane's upper arms as she clawed at him, grasped him, and pulled him down upon her.

Their coming together, at last, was shattering in its intensity. Their cries of ecstasy tangled with the song of the wolves, and was one with the primal music of the night.

CHAPTER TWENTY

DARKNESS LEACHED EVERY BIT OF WARMTH FROM the mountain. The air was brisk enough to sting the nostrils, and heavily laden with the scents of pine and moss, fertile earth. Blaze became slowly aware of the night around her as she rose lazily from the arms of sleep. She felt and breathed the cold, smelled the growing things. Then remembered why her heart was filled with such joy.

The memory passed through her entire body as a spasm of delight. From head to toe, she tingled. The sensation increased as she became aware of Bane pressed against her length, warm against her side. She became aware of what had pulled her from sleep.

He moved against her, so gently she wasn't certain if he twitched in the throes of a dream, or was slowly turning to his side. She only knew that the feel of him was glorious, wondrous. If he turned to her to love her again, to rouse her from sleep to passion, she would willingly, eagerly, open her arms to him. She was as open to Bane as a flower to sunlight and rain.

Blaze lifted a shoulder, prepared to meet him and welcome him with her body, ready to press her breast once more against his broad, smooth chest. But her world was turned suddenly, and violently, upside down.

One moment she was cocooned in blankets at her lover's side, anticipating the pleasures of their bodies; in the next the warmth was torn from her body as Bane shoved her roughly away from him. She rolled from the blankets onto the cold, damp grass, and gasped with the shock of it. An instant later her mind screamed in silent protest. What was wrong? Why was Bane treating her this way?

Blaze had no more time to think. Bane was abruptly on top of her, pressing her into the freezing earth. He wrapped his arms around her and rolled until it was she on top, then again, and she was on the bottom. What was happening? Panicked, Blaze tried to push him away, but his grip was like a band of iron about her wrist.

Which was loosened before she could find her voice to scream, and now Bane thrust away from her. She tried to rise, but he stopped her with a snarl.

"Don't move."

Terrified, Blaze watched Bane move into a crouch. Naked, he sidled, inch by inch, toward the tousled pile of clothing they had abandoned mere hours earlier. She watched him reach into the tangle, withdraw his knife . . .

Blaze's terror found its voice. She screamed. And the sound of it was drowned in the roar from the great, dark, shaggy grizzly that rose from all fours to challenge the trespassers who had crossed into his territory.

"Back, Blaze . . . get back."

She shrank away from the horror that towered over them, jaws gaping, slavering. Bane did not move from his crouch. Starlight glittered from the blade he held in his hand. The bear roared another angry challenge and dropped back down to the ground. A scream that Blaze did not recognize flew from her throat as the huge animal charged.

Bane leapt to one side at the last possible moment, and the grizzly rushed past. It wheeled as, in the same instant, Bane jumped sideways. He reached again into the tumbled pile of clothing, and his hand emerged with one of Blaze's pistols. But the bear was almost upon him. Stumbling backward, Bane fired.

Blaze became aware of several things all at once. She saw the muzzle flash from the pistol against the dark of the night; heard the terrified squeals of the horses; saw the beast wince as a bullet impacted somewhere in his massive form; heard Bane grunt as the animal engulfed him and bore him to the ground.

For a second Blaze remained frozen with shock and horror. Then the squealing of the horses penetrated her numbed brain. The horses . . . Bane's rifle in the saddle sheath.

The bear's enraged snarls were interrupted by a rumble of pain. Had Bane managed to get his blade into the animal? There was no way to tell. The bear embraced the man so tightly she could scarce tell one body from the other. Then she heard another voice cry out in pain. Bane's.

Blaze dove to the place where they had carefully laid their saddles on the ground. Her hands found the sheath. The grizzly roared again, and she saw Lonesome's pale body in the background. The horse reared and whinnied shrilly. Her fingers groped the wooden stock. The rifle was free and in her hands. She lifted it to her shoulder.

The animal had risen once more to his hind legs. He was crushing the life out of Bane. Blaze watched Bane's left hand stab ineffectually at the beast's chest. The pistol had dropped from his right. His knees buckled, and now only the bear's grasp kept him from falling.

Bane's body blocked a clean shot at the grizzly's

torso. There was only one place to aim, and only one chance to hit the target. Blaze sucked in her breath. The bear's claws raked down Bane's back, leaving torn and bloody trails. Bane's head lolled on his shoulders. Blaze let her breath out slowly as her finger tightened on the trigger. She fired.

CHAPTER TWENTY-ONE

THE SUN BEAT DOWN RELENTLESSLY THROUGH THE thin mountain air to warm Blaze's back, now long healed. Rivulets of sweat ran down from her temples to drip from her chin. She watched the drops darken the hide she examined for any sign of imperfection. Seeing nothing, she sat up straight and, laboriously, turned it over, fur-side up. She glanced at Bane.

Tears mingled with sweat. Blaze swiped at her nose with the back of her hand. "Bane," she called softly.

His profile remained turned to her, his gaze on a distant peak. He was motionless but for a barely perceptible tic working just above the jawline. Ever so slowly, he swiveled his gaze in her direction.

"I . . . I think I'm ready for the next step."

Silence. She watched his gaze flicker over the incipient robe in her lap. Tensing, she waited.

After several long moments, Bane unfolded from his cross-legged position on the ground and rose stiffly. It hurt her to watch him, although she knew he was healing, faster than she would have believed. When she had shot the bear, and finally managed to roll its corpse from his body, she hadn't believed he would live through the night. The wounds were hideous, long, deep troughs dug into the flesh of his back by the grizzly's claws. His loss of blood was profuse, frightening, and his bronze-toned skin had turned as white as snow.

But he had remained conscious and told her what to do, how to care for him. It was ironic, Blaze had thought, that only earlier that day he had been soothing the welts on her own back. Now she was tending to his, and trying to save his life. It had been a very long night, and even when dawn pinked the horizon she had still feared for his life. His pallor remained appalling; his eyes were closed, and she could not see the rise and fall of his chest. For one horrifying moment she thought he had slipped away from her. A soft cry had escaped her then, and his eyes opened slowly.

"Take . . . my knife," he had said, voice like the creak of a rusty hinge. "Skin it. I will . . . guide you. You will make a . . . cape . . . for the winter. When it is done I . . . I will be healed. We will leave."

Blaze had opened her mouth, but no words would

come. Skin the bear? Make a cape? How did he know how long that would take? How did he know he'd be healed . . . ?

Blaze remembered closing her mouth, pressing her lips together to stop her foolish questions. If Bane said it would be so, it would be so. She knelt beside him to reassure him, to tell him she would do as he asked, but his eyes had closed again. And this time she knew he slept. Deeply.

Bane's long shadow fell over her, and Blaze looked up, returning to the present. She hoped to catch his gaze, but it roved the bearskin, inspecting for flaws, perhaps. She looked away quickly, before he might see the damning tears building in her eyes.

Bane grunted and she recognized the sound. Approval. Grudging, but approval nonetheless. She heard his knees creak as he crouched beside her.

"Listen, and I will tell you what next to do . . ."

Blaze flexed her aching fingers, turned them over and examined them. She wasn't surprised to see the blisters in the fading light of the sun. The primitive bone needle and rawhide thread Bane had produced, once she had shaped the hide, had been difficult to work with. No wonder he'd told her he'd be ready to travel by the time she was done with the cape. At the rate she was going, it would be next year before she was finished.

Sighing, Blaze shoved the bulky skin from her lap, folded it, and laid it to the side. With the tip of her tongue, she attempted to fish out from between her teeth a piece of the dried meat that had been her dinner. Failing, she plucked at it with her fingers, one eye cocked on Bane. He paid her no attention. Would he ever look her way again with the desire in his eyes she had seen the night they had been attacked? Or had their interlude been just that . . . a moment out of time, a stop along the way? She had thought . . .

But, no. Blaze shook her head, scattering the traitorous thoughts. She had vowed not to dwell on what-might-have-beens, or even what she truly believed had existed between them. What good would it do? She must focus on her one goal, her one path. Bane had even spoken aloud the words that formed the stepping stones of that path.

The scarred man . . . He will be delivered to hell by you, Blaze of Lightning . . .

The scarred man.

Blaze forced her thoughts away from the here and now, from Bane, back into the past. One slow, agonizing step at a time she took herself back to her village. She ran through the gate, heard the screams, witnessed the carnage . . .

. . . saw his face. Looked into his eyes. Watched Tomas . . .

Harsh, bitter tears scalded her eyelids, slid down her cheeks. She didn't bother to wipe them away. Their heat ignited the embers that had been banked within her breast. The flames flickered to life, and she welcomed them.

Blaze took a deep breath as the renewed passion of her quest filled her, flowed through her limbs, consumed her. Something thick seemed to clog her throat, and she coughed.

From the corner of her eye, Blaze noticed Bane's head turn in her direction, but willed away the sudden emotional flutter. There was room in her life for only one emotion; she would do well to remember it. As it seemed Bane was doing.

A second quick glance assured Blaze of what she had expected. Bane had turned away from her, his gaze apparently focused on a distant white-capped peak. He did not blink, did not move. What was he thinking? Of her? Or of the road ahead?

It didn't matter. Not anymore. All there was, for either of them, was the road ahead.

It was long dark when Bane finally moved his gaze from the faraway horizon. He allowed his mind to relax its focus, let it flow throughout the rest of his body, bringing him alive again. He turned his head and let his eyes flick over the scene before him.

Blaze lay sleeping, curled around the bearskin. The remains of their fire crackled faintly in the nearly silent darkness, the only other sound a rustling in the treetops. Bane licked his lips, aware suddenly of his thirst. And hunger. He had denied himself too long.

Muscles flexed painfully when Bane rose to his feet, and there was a sharp twinge in his back as the skin stretched, but he welcomed the discomfort. It reminded him of something he must never forget again.

He had one goal, one purpose. To lose sight of it would mean failure. Just one small distraction had almost cost him his life. One small distraction . . .

Against his will, Bane was drawn once more to the sleeping figure. One small distraction.

Bane almost laughed. Immediately, he caught himself. It must be the white part of him, he thought with disgust. The part that valued life so little. The part he must put aside. Forever.

He straightened. Pushed past the pain in his back, his aching muscles. His hunger and thirst. Avoided another sideways look at the woman sleeping by the fire. She was trouble; he had known it from the first.

Trouble to his soul. To his future. To his purpose. He had known, but ignored it. He had seen the same fire in her that burned in him. He had felt union with her. And when he discovered they sought the same prey . . .

Unaware, Bane clenched his teeth. He needed her. That was a fact he knew in the very core of his soul. He needed, wanted her, with every fiber of his being.

But only to bring down the beast. The twin symbols of lightning would be brought together, and the resulting conflagration would consume the monster. Bane knew he must not be consumed as well. To touch her again, to be lured from his path again, would spell death. On an elemental level, he knew it.

Blinking away the vision of the woman curled around the bearskin, Bane turned on his heel and strode away into the night.

CHAPTER TWENTY-TWO

BLAZE'S AWAKENING SENSES TOLD HER IT WAS JUST before dawn. The chill was leaving the night air, and it touched her with a promise of warmth in the day to come. Dew-damp earth and the primal odors of wood and leafy foliage filled her nostrils. Any moment she would hear the first birdsong of the day. She turned over and momentarily buried her face in the fragrant mustiness of her bearskin.

Bane was already up. She heard him moving about their campsite. Minutes later she heard the crackle of a small fire. Blaze lifted her head and pushed her hair out of her eyes. Her brows arced.

"Is that a coffeepot I see?"

Bane merely grunted.

Blaze sat up and straightened her clothes, then raked her fingers through her hair. She watched her companion pull a skillet out of a pack and set it on the fire alongside the coffeepot.

"Is there something special about today?" Blaze asked.

Bane laid strips of bacon in the pan. Nodding with apparent satisfaction, he sat back on his haunches.

"Yes," he replied at length. "There is something special. It is another day we are alive."

Blaze's mouth watered as the smell of frying bacon and boiling coffee wafted in her direction. She allowed the trace of a smile to curl her lips as she rose from her bearskin bed and strode into the privacy of the surrounding trees. When she returned, she sat across the fire from Bane and accepted the tin cup of coffee he offered her.

"Thank you," she said simply. Their eyes met briefly. Neither flinched away, and Blaze breathed a short, inward sigh of relief.

Things were better. It was a long time coming, but things had improved. Ever since . . .

Blaze turned away and fingered the coarse, dense hair of the skin she had cured herself. *"When it is done, I . . . I will be healed. We will leave."*

And so they had. She finished the hide late one afternoon. The sun was partially hidden behind the distant peak, its slanting rays setting diamonds in the shrinking snowcap. It was almost eerily silent at the lakeside, not even the scolding of a jay. The perfume of pine enveloped her. Then a trout jumped, its splash startling her. She didn't hear the footfall behind her, and was only aware of Bane's presence when his shadow fell over her.

"It is done," he stated quietly.

Blaze glanced down at the cape in her lap. Yes. It was done. Wrapped in the comfortable numbness of the afternoon's serenity, she forgot the finishing touches she earlier completed. She replied without glancing up at Bane.

"I've . . . I've done everything you told me."

"And it is well done," he said so softly she wasn't certain she heard. When she turned around, he was gone, as silently as he arrived.

When she awoke the next morning, Bane had packed their modest camp. The horses were tacked and ready to ride. Watching Bane mount, Blaze saw his stiffness, the lingering edges of pain. It was amazing he could mount at all, much less ride. She had not thought he would live, and when he survived she had not thought he would heal. But then, she hadn't thought she could skin the bear either, much less craft the skin.

Or bury her entire village.

The now-familiar hot tide surged through her veins, warming her body, steeling her heart, cocooning her from pain and heartache.

Blaze's gaze flicked briefly over Bane. He sat erect in his saddle, staring into the distance, the path they would travel. He held the reins loosely, forearms crossed over the pommel, waiting for her. She readied herself quickly, greeted her horse with a brisk neck rub, and climbed into the saddle. Bane started off without a word. He never looked back.

The days on the trail had been long and hard. And lonely. Blaze almost felt she had ceased to exist. Certainly what happened between them faded into nothingness as if it, too, did not exist, had never occurred. Reality became surreal, dreamlike. There was only the endless, dusty road winding down from the mountains toward the plains beyond. And then they ran into a group of settlers headed south out of the Wyoming area.

Initial greetings were reluctant and stilted. A grizzled, weather-beaten old man, obviously the leader, eyed them warily, slitted gaze taking in their buckskins and black, braided hair. When it appeared he wasn't about to be overtly hostile, Bane asked if he'd heard any rumors of trouble on the trail.

"Yeah," the old man replied grudgingly from his wagon bench. "Heard 'bout some trouble 'round Laramie."

Bane's posture never changed, but Blaze knew he

was instantly and keenly alert. He nodded his encouragement to the old man.

"Don't know much. We was south o' the fort. Just heard 'bout some gang o' marauders. Bad 'uns."

The quirk of an eyebrow conveyed Bane's question.

"Cain't tell ya much more. Didn't stick 'round t'find out. Got women with us, y'know?" He cast a lewd eye on Blaze's body. "Or mebbe ya don't know. Squaws is different, ain't they? More like . . . animals."

Bane never even blinked although Blaze knew every muscle in his body was tensed. Slowly, ever so slowly, he sat back in the saddle, leather creaking, and straightened his spine.

"Good day to you, then. And good luck," he said.

The threat implied in the mere tone of his voice was as chilling as the hiss of a venomous snake. Blaze watched the old man pale under his leathery tan.

Bane kicked his horse into a lope and Blaze followed. She didn't look back, but heard the lead driver crack his whip sharply. The sound of rapid hoofbeats told her they had abruptly quickened their ambling pace south, and she smiled inwardly with grim satisfaction.

Despite her burning curiosity, Blaze did not try to breach the wall Bane had erected by questioning him about the "trouble" near Laramie. She guessed it was partly pride, partly fear of his response. No matter how hard she tried to deny it, no matter the poisoned

211

memories she deliberately pumped into her veins to shield her from the pain, his rejection went to her core. The wound was still raw.

But the atmosphere seemed somewhat thawed this morning. Blaze accepted the proffered plate of bacon and dry, hard, trail biscuit. She looked up at Bane from under lowered brows.

"Bane?"

The nearly imperceptible widening of one eye was her only response. She interpreted it as an invitation to continue.

"That old man the other day, the one who talked about trouble near Laramie . . ."

"The Sioux nations gather there for the summer," he replied to her unfinished question, "as I told you. Like any group, any herd, they attract predators sniffing out the weak."

"You think the scarred man—"

"Yes," he said curtly. "The carrion eaters will also come."

"But, do you think he has anything to do with the trouble? With this gang?"

Bane's shoulders twitched in what might have been a shrug. "I know what you know."

"And where there's a stink, you'll find garbage."

Was that a smile she saw trying to curl the corners of his mouth? A light in his eye?

"I'm starting to sound like you, aren't I?"

His teeth flashed white in his bronzed face. He allowed the smile to linger while he kicked dirt on their fire. Blaze helped him pack up the camp, and in nearly perfect unison they swung onto their horses. She noticed while the smile had vanished, so had the almost-constant tension in Bane's shoulders. He put his heels to his mare, then as abruptly halted her. He turned to Blaze.

"His name is Jake," he said simply.

"Jake," she repeated, overcoming the urge to spit. "A dead man's name."

Bane's lips remained a straight, compressed line. But the light had returned to his eyes. Blaze let herself sink into their blue depths.

Like summer lightning, the thing between them sizzled. Life flowed through her veins again. And passion. The passion for revenge.

As one, they urged their mounts into a lope. Only a fading cloud of dust marked their passage through the trees and onto the long, long road.

CHAPTER TWENTY-THREE

IT WAS ALMOST NOON AND THE SUN WAS HIGH AND hot. Carrie's horse was dark with sweat, and her shirt was plastered to her back. Pushing back strands of strawberry blond hair escaped from her twin braids, she reined in her sorrel and looked around.

The tree-clad mountains surrounded her with undeniable majesty. Although she had grown up in Wyoming, the secluded, wild beauty of the area never failed to awe and inspire her. She heard from travelers who bought the occasional horse from her parents that the forested mountains to the north and west were even more magnificent. But Carrie liked where she was just fine. She watched a hawk make a lazy circle downslope from her position, then headed into the valley to her favorite spot by the stream.

Her sense of well-being increased when she dismounted, hobbled her gelding, and opened the modest lunch her mother had packed for her. Squatting in the shade of a cottonwood tree beside the water, she pulled a slice of buttered bread and an apple from her pack.

She should start back soon. There was no sign of the small band of mares she had spotted earlier in the day. She had been able to track them up into the foothills but had lost them when they apparently headed up the scree from a rockfall. Not that she had much chance of catching up to them anyway. Carrie smiled to herself.

Horses were smarter than most people gave them credit for. She loved and appreciated them, as did her parents. Occasionally it was hard to sell some of them. But it was their livelihood, and she loved caring for them. And she loved the excuse to take off in the middle of the day simply for another glimpse of the wild band. She remembered the twinkle in her father's gray eyes when they realized simultaneously what caused the approaching dust cloud. He put down the food bucket and turned to her.

"We'll be able to see 'em in a minute."

And then there they were, tails flagged as they flew over the dusty ground, fleeing from something real or imagined, heading for the foothills to the northwest. Carrie felt an excited chill run down her spine. One of the mares was a bay with stockings and a blaze, a standout in the herd. Carrie sighed audibly with appreciation.

"Why don'cha saddle up and follow 'em a way? See what you can see."

Carrie's heart beat a little faster. She turned to her mother who stood over the washtub, round cheeks rosy from exertion. Lydia Olssen nodded indulgently and swiped a strand of pale blond hair, now nearly white, from her forehead.

There was no way she would ever catch up to the band; it was only the joy of the ride that mattered. Still, she hesitated.

"Go on, now," her mother said, love in her voice. "You worked hard this mornin'."

It was all the encouragement she needed. Without a word, she quickly tacked her favorite saddle horse and took off at a gallop.

A soft whicker from her sorrel drew Carrie's attention, and she pushed to her feet. It was time to go back and help her parents with the afternoon chores. Maybe tomorrow she'd take a little time and look for the herd again. Just for the joy of the ride, of course.

The sun had started its downward arc when Carrie crested a last ridge and saw the modest house with its three corrals, small barn, and thriving vegetable garden. She didn't see her parents, however, which was odd. Her mother should be out hanging the laundry she was doing when Carrie left, and her father was almost always doing something with the horses. There were only four of them at the moment, but . . .

At the moment there were five; a horse she had never seen before, looking hard-ridden, was tied to the porch railing.

Carrie's heart caught in her throat. Something was wrong. She just knew it.

The sorrel responded at once to the pressure of his rider's heels. Half-sliding down the remainder of the slope, he hit level ground and broke immediately into a lope. Carrie leaned low on his neck, gently urging him to greater speed.

The house grew larger in her vision. She could see the front door was open. A bleached muslin curtain puffed out an open window with the vagrant breeze, and relaxed inside again, as if the house breathed. Terror seized her by the throat. An instant later it started to strangle.

A stranger walked out the front door. He hitched up his pants, spit to the side, then caught sight of her. His hand went to the gun at his hip.

Carrie hauled on the reins, and the sorrel came to a skidding halt. The stranger pulled his gun and, with a slow, evil smile, pointed it at her.

"Come on, girlie," he drawled. "Get down off that horse. Let's you an' me have a party."

Frozen with horror, only Carrie's eyes moved. Her gaze flicked back to the front door. The stranger laughed.

"Ain't no one in there kin help you. Get down, now. Get down."

His voice had hardened. The smile was gone. He cocked the hammer.

She had practically been born on a horse. She trusted her skills. Carrie wheeled the sorrel and put her heels to his sides. Hard.

A pistol shot rang out.

If she was hit, she felt nothing. She kept riding. With a second set of hoofbeats now pounding behind her.

"Well, Ring, I think yer crazy t'change yer plans, but I ain't gonna complain about the scenery." Sandy tipped his hat to an attractive young woman hurrying along the raised wooden walkway. She looked away, cheeks blazing, and when she'd passed, he hurried to catch up with Ring and Rowdy, spurs clanking.

"I don't know what part of my new plan you think is crazy," Ring replied. "I thought it was pretty sharp, m'self."

"But you *know* you can sell them horses in Missouri."

"Most likely." Ring stepped off the sidewalk and headed across the street. He stopped and waited for an ox-drawn wagon to pass, then continued. "Most likely I can sell 'em to the army in Fort Laramie, too. 'Sides, Wyoming's closer than Missouri."

Rowdy rolled his eyes. He'd heard the question, and the reply, more times than he could count. Sandy hadn't shut up about their change of direction since Ring made the decision. Pushing the brim of his hat up, he followed Ring through the swinging saloon doors. Didn't Sandy realize there was more to their boss's change of plans than met the eye? Ring asked for news and rumor wherever they stopped, and wasn't there rumor of trouble up in northern Wyoming? Not to mention tales of an odd bounty-hunting couple, a Mexican gal and a half breed.

Ring strolled up to the bar, removed his hat, slapped the dust off on his thigh, and leaned against the polished surface.

The bartender smiled, the corners of his mouth disappearing into fat cheeks. "What's your pleasure?"

The men ordered, and when they had their drinks he inquired about a hotel. Finishing his beer and armed with information, he threw a few coins on the counter. And heard the shouts and the thunder of galloping hooves. A runaway? He pushed away from the bar and headed for the door, Sandy and Rowdy in his wake. When he heard a woman's agonized shriek for help, he broke into a trot.

Carrie was only dimly aware she could no longer hear the hoofbeats following her. It did not occur to her the pursuer must have veered off when she neared and entered the town. She knew merely she was chased by a man who pointed a gun at her . . . and fired. Beyond that—her parents, what the stranger was doing in their house—she could not think. She could only ride.

And then the town was all around her, enfolding her, saving her. She saw people on the sidewalks pass by in a blur. She sped past a couple of single riders and a wagon. A voice she didn't recognize as hers erupted from her throat, calling for help.

Others shouted at her, yelled at her to pull up, stop her horse. Panic ebbed, and she leaned back in her saddle, keeping constant pressure on the reins. The sorrel slowed to a trot, sides heaving, and Carrie started to shake. Then the exhausted horse went to his knees.

Ring arrived at exactly the right moment. A rangy sorrel, lathered and over-ridden, collapsed, and his rider lurched forward. Ring caught her and pulled her away from the distressed animal before he could roll over on her leg. Once he had her steadied, he swooped her up into his arms.

Huge blue eyes stared at him from a pale and pretty face peppered with freckles. As he watched, the eyes filled with tears and he became aware of the girl's trembling. An instant later, she burst into sobs and buried her face in his chest. Aware of all the curious stares and muttered questions, Ring turned on his heel and carried her inside the saloon.

A dog's tail of onlookers followed. Sandy rushed ahead and pulled out a chair at one of the round tables and Ring tried to set the girl down, but she clung to him stubbornly, still weeping. With a sigh, he sat in the chair himself. Awkwardly, he patted her back.

"Come on, now, miss, calm down. Calm down and tell me what happened. Can't help if you don't tell me what's wrong."

A moment later she looked up at him, hiccoughing. Strands of strawberry blond hair, escaped from two long braids, streaked her flushed cheeks and clung to her sweat-damp neck.

"A . . . a stranger," she stammered. "I was out riding, and I . . . I came home, but . . . but someone was there . . . coming out of my house . . ."

Ring tensed. He glanced quickly at Sandy and Rowdy, then back to the girl. "Go on," he encouraged.

Carrie took a deep breath. "He told me to get down. He . . ." The tears welled again. "I knew what he wanted," she whispered. "I stayed on my horse. Then he pulled a gun . . ."

Subtly, Ring began to ease the girl off his lap. There was a murmuring in the crowd, and a stocky man with a badge made his way to the table.

"What's going on here?" he demanded. "What happened, Carrie?"

Carrie rose to unsteady feet and repeated what she had just told Ring.

"Where're your parents?" he asked tersely.

Carrie's face crinkled, but she managed to find her voice. "In . . . inside, I think. I didn't see them."

Ring stood and nodded at Sandy and Rowdy. The three made their way toward the saloon doors. The sheriff caught up with them, giving orders as he shoved ahead and out into the street.

"Ed, Mitchell, go find Frank. We're riding out to the Olssen farm. Get anybody else who'll come along. I don't like the sound of this."

"We'll come," Ring said quickly. "Me and one of my men."

The sheriff nodded curtly. "You got horses?"

"Sure do."

"Then come along. And thank you."

"Wait!" Carrie shoved her way to the sheriff's side. "I'm going with you."

Ring and the sheriff exchanged glances over the

top of her head.

"Carrie, I don't think—"

"They're my *parents*."

"Your horse is done, Carrie, and we're wasting time." The sheriff turned abruptly away.

"Mister!" Carrie whirled on Ring. "Please. I *have* to go with you. You can't leave me behind."

Ring opened his mouth to protest, but Carrie was too quick.

"You said there were two of you. Please let me have one of your horses. *Please.*"

The sheriff and two others were already mounted. Ring made up his mind. And hoped he wouldn't regret it.

"Sandy, give her your horse."

"Ring! I—"

"Just do it."

Scant minutes later the riders left the town behind in a fading cloud of dust. Ring rode easily, almost lazily, reins loosely gripped in one hand. He watched the girl from the corner of one eye.

Although her features were deeply etched with lines of fear, she was a pretty little thing, with a pretty little figure, despite the camouflage of men's clothing. She could ride, too, he noted with appreciation. But he felt bad for her. The scenario she had described did not bode well for a positive outcome.

Ring's apprehension deepened as they approached the homestead. Four horses stood in a corral, heads down, tails swishing. There was not another sign of life. No one came to the door to inquire about the din of approaching riders. They dismounted in front of the house.

The sheriff drew his gun and approached the porch cautiously. Ring hung back, his eye on the girl. He watched what little color remained in her face drain away when the sheriff called out and no one replied. The sheriff, the others behind him, entered the front door. Ring moved to the girl's side.

Too soon the sheriff emerged, shaking his head. He took his hat off when he approached Carrie. But it was Ring she turned to.

Her expression was stricken, her fingers curled into the frozen imitation of talons. Ring took her gently by the shoulders.

"Carrie," he said, using her name for the first time, personalizing the moment for all time, taking her pain and tragedy as his burden. "This man, the stranger . . . do you remember at all what he looked like?"

She nodded mutely. Then she raised a finger to the side of her head and ran it down her cheek. "He had a scar," she breathed. "A scar . . ."

CHAPTER TWENTY-FOUR

It seemed as if her former life, her childhood, was very, very far away. Her family, everyone she loved, were encased in a bubble that floated above her like a tag-along dream. The desert she had grown up in was like someone else's distant memory; she remembered the description of it as though the details had been related to her. She saw it in her mind's eye, but had lost the feel of it.

What was real was the creak of saddle leather day after day after day, forested mountain slopes and the trails in between. The bearskin beneath her in the cool of the night, the feel of buckskin against her flesh, and the summer sun beating on her shoulders through the increasingly long days. The blaze of hatred that seared her soul driving her onward, ever onward . . . and the man who rode at her side.

As if able to sense the least movement of her body, including the slightest shift of her eyes, Bane's gaze met hers at the instant she glanced his way. Though his lips did not relay it, there was a smile for her in his soul. It was enough, and she was content.

The day wore on toward evening, and Bane finally called a halt to camp for the night. He had found a patch of relatively flat ground on a low ridge in the foothills of a building mountain range with a protective stand of trees. The vantage point was good; no one could approach without being seen and heard. It was a position they found increasingly important to maintain.

Blaze worked at Bane's side, as she did at every campsite, until it was time to light the fire. They didn't always have one. Some nights they chewed on jerky and took turns keeping watch in the darkness. The men they hunted, successfully, learned to fear them, and they were hunted in turn.

Watching Bane arrange the fuel within the ring of stones, Blaze lowered herself to the ground and leaned back against her saddle, inhaling the pleasant fragrance of the new leather. Idly, she ran a finger over the back of the cantle, following the elaborate tooling that scrolled a fanciful design. She heard Bane chuckle softly.

"You like your new saddle," he said, squatting to light the fire.

"Very much. But I really didn't need a new saddle."

"No. The old one was good. Well worn and comfortable." Bane blew on the small flicker in the heart of the tinder. It caught and a flame licked upward.

"But we have to spend all that money on something, don't we?" Blaze grinned.

Bane sank back onto his haunches and pulled his pack over to him. "New skillet," he announced, and slid it onto the fire. "Beans, coffee, flour, sugar, bacon, cornmeal, salt, and lard."

Blaze's eyes widened and she sat upright. "When did you get all that?"

"When you were looking at that saddle." With fluid grace he rose and crossed to the pile he had made of his own saddle, colorful saddle blanket, bedroll, and brand-new rifle sheath. He pulled out the gun and rested it against his shoulder. "I'll be back by full dark. You know how to make cornbread?"

"Do you know how to shoot?"

His expression never changed. It didn't have to. When he disappeared over the crest of the ridge, Blaze threw a small handful of lard into the hot skillet. As it popped and sizzled, she was suddenly pulled away from the moment, the present, back to a time she had thought she would never experience again.

Blaze stood beside her mother and the smooth river rock heating over the cook fire. Laughing at something her daughter had said to her, she threw a bit of fat on the rock. While it crackled and spit, Louisa watched her expertly form the tortilla, throwing it up and catching it again on the back of her fists until it was the perfect shape . . .

A single tear falling on her forearm brought Blaze sharply back to reality. She shook her head and longed for the moment she experienced earlier in the day, the moment she had felt the blissful disconnection. When only the anger had mattered, not the pain.

It returned to her by the time Bane came striding over the ridge crest, rifle on one shoulder, a brace of squirrels swung over the other. He sniffed her cornbread appreciatively and set to work skinning the fruits of his hunt. In no time at all they were spitted, salted, and roasting over the fire. The relative peace remained until she sucked the last of her dinner from her fingertips.

Bane threw his bones into the fire and swiped his mouth with the back of his hand. He looked across the fire at Blaze.

"We will not take another man as we did the last ones."

The statement took her so completely by surprise she wasn't sure at first what Bane was talking about. Her lips parted with an unformed, unasked question as her eyebrows made twin question marks. Then it hit her.

"Bane, it . . . it worked out fine. We caught them. We got the bounty."

Bane didn't reply at once. A muscle jumped at his jawline. His eyes unfocused, as if he looked at something far away. Then, suddenly, he returned his attention to her.

"Listen to me. We will not tempt a man, or fate, again that way."

Blaze caught her bottom lip in her teeth, understanding Bane. And remembering.

There were three of them, men wanted for a series of stagecoach robberies. They had even raped a female passenger and cold-bloodedly murdered her husband. She and Bane had seen the wanted poster in northern Colorado and had spoken with the sheriff in a nearby town. The men had a hiding place in the mountains, they learned. A good one. No one had been able to track them down. No one, until Bane and Blaze rode into the foothills.

It had been so easy, a tactic she employed the very first time she had earned a bounty. The only difference was she had Bane to back her up this time.

They had easily disguised themselves as an itinerant brave and his sullen squaw. It wasn't long before they were set upon. Blaze smiled grimly to herself.

She had wanted to go alone into the hills. It was

safer, she thought, to have Bane shadow her and take down the bandits when they accosted her. But he had been adamant.

"We ride together. Or not at all."

She knew him well. She knew the hard core of him, the part as hard as the heart of the ironwood tree. She had acquiesced silently.

And so they rode from the little northern Colorado town, dying as the mines it fed played out, on horses rented from the livery stable. Their own mounts would have given them away immediately.

Four days they wandered, seemingly aimlessly, through the rugged, dry foothills. They hunted to feed themselves. By night Blaze hunkered by the fire, playing the downtrodden squaw, cooking and cleaning up their meager leavings. It would have rankled but for the fact they knew they were watched. They had thrown out the bait, and the scent had drifted to their quarry.

On the fifth day, Blaze was saddle weary. Not from action, but inaction. All day they plodded, small spurts of dust rising from beneath their horses' hooves. Only the creak of harness leather competed with the occasional cry of a circling hawk. Blaze wondered if perhaps the men had moved on, that the feeling of being watched was purely a figment of her imagination.

And then they heard the click of shod hooves

against rocks, and the tumbling of stones down a slope, and the grunt of men jarred in their saddles. No attempt at stealth was made at all. One moment they were alone; the next they faced three riders.

The men, unshaven apparently for weeks, greasy hair hanging to their shoulders beneath sweat-stained hats, grinned wickedly. One licked his lips lasciviously.

"Hand over the squaw, Injun," the skinniest, and dirtiest, of the trio commanded. "Hand 'er over an' we might let y'live."

They were already reaching for their sidearms.

A bad feeling clenched the pit of her belly. It was what she'd feared.

Blaze saw the tension in Bane, saw his back muscles bunch, saw the twitch in his forearm. The bad guys saw nothing.

And had nothing to fear. Not yet, anyway. She knew Bane would let the scene play out, waiting for his moment to strike.

But she didn't like it. They needn't have simply walked into the lion's jaws. Why did Bane have to force it? Why did he have to put them in the position where violence was ultimately the only solution?

As soon as she asked the silent question, she knew. From beneath lowered lashes, almost lazily, as if fate had already treated her so badly she had nothing left to fear, Blaze studied the men.

They were not only filthy, their eyes were flat and vacant. There was nothing in them, nothing left, no hope, charity, dreams. They were dead. All that remained was the manner of their deaths. They were like the others, the ones who had taken her life away. She had seen the same look in their eyes, too.

Earlier in the day she had felt the pain again. But only for a little while. The painful moments were fewer, less frequent. Someday, perhaps, they would be gone forever. Replaced by . . . this.

It surged in her powerfully, as she knew it moved through Bane. She understood, knew why he wanted it to bring it to this point, this culmination. Knew why he did not fear for her as long as he was with her.

He was invincible with the power of it running in his blood. As she was.

"Hey. Hey, you." The one on the left gestured with his gun. "Move over there. Move away from that squaw."

Bane straightened slowly in the saddle.

"An' while yer at it," he added, "how 'bout handin' over that rifle? What's a no count Injun like you doin' with a nice piece like 'at anyhows?"

The three laughed as if they had just heard a very funny joke. Bane slowly drew the rifle from its sheath and handed it to the man on the nearest horse. Blaze resisted the impulse to draw in her breath sharply.

"'At's more like it." The man briefly admired the rifle, holding it up in one hand. Then he tossed it to the rider next to him. "Now move away from that squaw, like I said 'afore." His voice turned into a snarl.

Bane obligingly, and with the outward appearance of fear, moved his mount to the side.

"Now get over here, squaw."

As tightly drawn as a bowstring, Blaze put her heels to her horse's sides.

"Wait."

All four paused for a second, attention returned to Bane.

"Get down, woman," he growled at Blaze. "The horse is mine."

A tense silence followed. Then one of the men snorted with laughter.

It was the moment she had waited for, the one she knew Bane would create. Obediently, she swung her right leg behind her, over the back of her saddle. She knew all eyes were on her. Knew Bane reached for the pistol slipped into the back of his boot.

Two of the men were dead by the time she had both feet on the ground. Stunned by the sound of the gunfire, the third man gaped, momentarily frozen. He didn't even register Blaze's hand moving to the waistband of her buckskins. He, too, was dead an instant later.

Blaze found herself smiling inwardly as she stared into the dwindling flames of their campfire. It was neither a smile of happiness, nor contentment, but satisfaction maybe. Yes. Satisfaction. The men had been wanted dead or alive. They were better off dead. The world was better off. As it was better off without all the others they had brought in.

The faint crackling of the dying fire was the only sound in the cool, still darkness. Earlier an owl had hooted, and there was a rustling nearby in the forest undergrowth, but all was still as a half moon crept above the treetops. Blaze gazed over at Bane, and realized he had been watching her.

"Your thoughts have been far away," he commented quietly.

"Not so far."

"You were remembering."

"Yes." Blaze nodded. She watched a now-familiar, barely perceptible line form between his dark brows. It was the only part of his expression that changed. She awaited his next words.

"As I said, we will not do it that way again. I don't like using you as . . . bait."

"And as I said before," Blaze countered gently, "it worked out fine. Just like it did the other times."

Bane's light eyes seemed to gray, as if with smoke. "Those times are over, Blaze. I will not risk your safety in that way again."

"But, Bane," Blaze said, spine straightening with her jolt of surprise. "You're always with me. You—"

"Yes, I am always with you." Bane abruptly uncurled from his reclining position against his saddle and rose. "And I wish you always to be with me," he continued enigmatically.

Blaze felt her jaw drop, powerless to move the muscles to snap it shut again. She tried to speak, but was unable. She stared at Bane's back as he walked away from the fire. The tension in his shoulders and the stiffness of his stride told her as clearly as words he had something else to say. Heart pounding, she watched him turn back in her direction.

"Sleep, Blaze. We rise before dawn tomorrow."

Her only reply was an arch of her brows. It was the only response she could muster. And then it hit her.

"You know something you haven't told me," Blaze stated flatly.

He remained immobile and silent for a long moment. He blinked slowly, and Blaze watched his jaw work as he visibly tried to control himself.

"I have heard a rumor," he said at last. He had not wanted to tell her. Not yet. But he had not wanted to say the other thing either, the thing that constantly threatened to betray him. His need for her. His want.

"There are some very bad men, north of here,"

Bane continued. "Near Fort Laramie. The evil they do . . . reminds me . . ."

The flush of warmth that had recently raced through her veins turned to icy water. "Bane . . ."

But he had already disappeared into the darkness.

CHAPTER TWENTY-FIVE

ALTHOUGH RING WAS ANXIOUS TO REACH HIS DES-tination, he liked the comfort of Duchess's easy jog. Besides, he didn't want to use her up. Carrie might want to go for a ride with him. Ring looked back at the horse on the lead rope.

He sure hoped it would make her happy. She'd had precious little to smile about lately. Especially when he told her the news he was bringing. Frowning, he pulled his hat lower on his forehead. Funny, how important that seemingly small thing had become to him recently—Carrie's smile.

Forgetting the decision he'd made mere seconds ago, Ring kicked his mare into a slow lope as if he might run away from the disturbingly uneasy thought. It wasn't long before the modest homestead came into sight, a spiral of dust rising from one of the circular corrals.

Ring whoa-ed Duchess, and she stopped suddenly. Halting less abruptly, the horse on the lead drew even with the bay mare, then dropped his head to nibble at the sparse grass. Ring took his hat off and slapped it against his thigh.

It would be nice to surprise her, he thought. Might make the smile just that much wider. Besides, he had her horse so well trained it would be kinda fun to show it off.

Ring swung down off of Duchess and let his reins fall straight down. Like all his best mounts, she was trained to "ground tie." He led the second horse a few strides away and dropped the lead rope.

Immediately, the gelding lowered his head and cocked a rear leg in an attitude of relaxation. He was almost as good as tied to a fence post. Ring stroked his neck, patted him on his well-rounded rump, and turned back to his mare.

Gathering up the reins, he swung back into the saddle and kicked her into a lope. A quick look back over his shoulder assured him he'd turned out another expertly trained mount. The gelding remained where he was, only his erect and expressive ears indicating his interest in their departure. Otherwise, he didn't move a muscle. Ring turned his attention back to the little farmstead.

Carrie looked up from the horse she was grooming when she heard the sound of hoofbeats. The shadow of a smile touched the corners of her mouth and her heart lightened a little, recognizing the familiar lean and lanky form occupying the saddle. She untied the gelding she'd been working on, removed his halter, and let the horse rejoin his corralmates. She went out through the gate and awaited her company, halter and lead rope hung on her left arm.

Ring slowed when he watched Carrie leave the corral, mindful of the dust cloud he brought with him. He removed his hat, holding it to his chest, as he walked Duchess in her direction. His heart did that funny little squeeze thing when he saw the faint but pretty smile on her lips. But his spirits fell when he remembered what he had to tell her.

"Hello, Ring," Carrie said in greeting. "Any news?"

His heart dropped to his feet. Repositioning his hat on his head, he climbed off of Duchess and stood in front of Carrie looking her directly in the eye. Slowly, he nodded. He kept his expression rigidly sober so she would not, even for an instant, get her hopes up. It saddened him when he watched the tiny smile fade away entirely.

"They lost the trail, Carrie," Ring said at last. "I'm sorry."

Her lower lip quivered, and she quickly brought a hand to her mouth to stifle it. She turned away.

"No . . . no idea at all where he might have headed," she managed at last.

"North is all. At least, that's where he was headed when they lost him. He could be anywhere now."

Still staring into the distance, Carrie nodded.

"Someone'll catch up with 'im sooner or later." Ring tried to sound comforting, but his words sounded merely empty. "Sheriff made up a Wanted poster, dead or alive," he tried again. "Raised a five-hundred-dollar bounty already. Your parents were . . . were real well liked, Carrie."

Another brief nod.

"Sandy, Rowdy, and me, we . . . we, uh, put in a few dollars."

Carrie turned finally. Tears sparkled at the corners of her eyes. "Thank you, Ring," she breathed.

He firmed his lips, dipped his chin, and looked away himself. Why was this so hard?

"Would you . . . would you like to come in? I could make some coffee."

Ring almost accepted before he caught himself. "Mebbe in awhile. Carrie, I . . . I got a surprise for you. Somethin' I thought might cheer you up a mite."

Ring was rewarded with a return of her half smile and a slight widening of her eyes. Reddish brows arched.

"A surprise? For me?"

"Sure. Why not?" Ring felt his own smile trying to break out.

"Well . . ." Carrie tried to look around behind him, as if he might be hiding something in his back pocket. A smile emerged full blown.

"Nothin's back there 'cept my sorry, skinny backside," Ring teased.

"Then where?"

Her nose wrinkled when she smiled that wide. Ring put two fingers to his lips and whistled.

Carrie's piquant features molded into an expression of surprise. A fraction of a second later, she heard the familiar sound. Even more puzzled, she turned into the direction it seemed to come from. Her jaw dropped.

The gelding cantered lazily, but steadily, lead rope dragging. Nearing the pair, he dropped into a trot, halting directly in front of Ring.

"Oh, my . . . my gosh," Carrie whispered. "He's beautiful. I've never . . . never seen one like him before."

"He's called a pelouse." Ring patted the horse's white neck, and ran his palm over the animal's back to his spotted hindquarters. "The Nez Perce breed 'em, and I . . . I've taken a liking to them."

"I can see why." Moving to the other side of the horse, Carrie ran her hands over his compact, muscular body. Suddenly, she looked up sharply. "This . . .

this isn't the surprise, is it?"

"Sure is." Ring grinned. "Like 'im?"

Carrie's mouth opened, but no words emerged. She was speechless.

"Well? Do you?"

The tears reappeared. "You can't mean it," Carrie said, voice barely audible.

"I sure as heck don't know why not. I'm a horse trader, got plenty of 'em, and can do whatever I like with 'em, I guess."

Carrie shook her head slowly. "I . . . I don't think I can accept a gift like this, Ring. I . . . it's too much."

"Too much of what?" Ring's expression abruptly sobered. Though he tried real hard not to, he couldn't help remembering another girl, another spotted horse, and a part of him that still hurt. "Too much money? Too much friendliness?" He was sorry as soon as the words were out. But it was too late. He gazed down bleakly at Carrie.

Carrie started to protest, but shut her mouth. Something in Ring's eyes, a fleeting shadow perhaps, tugged at her heart. Then she saw the pain there, and the immediate attempt to cover it up. Barely aware of what she was doing, she laid a hand on his arm.

"It's just that no one's ever been this nice to me before, Ring," she said softly. "I guess I just don't know what to say. Or what to do, for that matter."

Ring glanced at the slender hand touching his arm. Before she could pull away, he covered her long, slim fingers with his calloused palm.

"My suggestion," he said gently, "would be to take the horse. I put some time into him. For you, Carrie."

There. He'd said it. It was out. Cringing inwardly, he tried not to envision a girl with long, black hair. And tried not to imagine what it would feel like when Carrie pulled her hand away and firmly turned down his gift.

She did neither. Rather, Carrie became hyperaware of the hard slope of muscle in Ring's upper arm, and the clean man scent of him, saddle leather and soap. Feeling a little breathless, she dropped her hand and broke the contact only reluctantly. She took a step away from him, and smiled.

"I think the first thing I should do is say 'thank you.' Then I can take the horse."

Ring let out the long exhalation of relief before he could stop himself. There was a moment of embarrassed silence, then both of them burst out laughing.

"Say, you . . . you think you'd like to go for a ride? Try out your new horse?"

"I can't think of anything I'd rather do."

It was true. She couldn't. Or, at least, she thought

she couldn't. Until Ring took her hand.

"Come on. I'll help you tack 'im up."

Side by side, still holding hands, they led their horses toward the corral.

CHAPTER TWENTY-SIX

AFTERNOON SUNLIGHT SLANTING THROUGH THE DIRTY window warmed a spot on the wood-planked floor. Blaze thought she could see the faint, dusty imprint of a boot heel. She concentrated on it. Tried to find its form and shape and lose herself in it. Only for a moment. Only until her blood stopped boiling. She kept her eyes on the floor when the sheriff's voice drilled into her head again.

"Frankly, I'm reluctant to talk to you at all. Maybe it'd be best if you just kept on moving."

Blaze didn't dare look at Bane. She shifted her gaze to the window. Heard him take a long, slow breath. Then the rustle of paper.

"These men are wanted," Bane said calmly. "Dead. Or alive."

Blaze's eyes flickered. In the periphery of her vision

she saw Bane holding the Wanted notice. The bottom half of it was crumpled in his white-knuckled fist.

"And if you and your . . . squaw woman go after 'em, they'll be dead fer sure."

The fury in Blaze uncoiled. She whipped around to face the short, portly sheriff with the ridiculous bald spot behind a short fringe of bangs. If it weren't for the heat of her anger, she might have laughed.

"I'm Mexican, Sheriff," she said tightly.

He didn't acknowledge her statement in the slightest way. Neither did Bane. But she saw a familiar tic jump.

"If it is not acceptable to bring these men in dead, then you should not publicize it so widely," Bane continued smoothly. He laid the notice carefully on the sheriff's desktop and smoothed it flat again. "I found this posted almost sixty miles from here. It was one of many I have seen."

The sheriff looked away and nervously licked his lips. "All I'm sayin' is . . . you got a reputation, y'know?"

"Yes, we know." Bane glanced briefly at Blaze. "A reputation for bringing to an end the crime sprees of some very bad men."

The sheriff cleared his throat. "Well, now, I'll . . . I'll admit that's true."

As the sheriff rubbed his chin, Bane stabbed his finger on the notice six times. "These six men have robbed white settlers."

The sheriff nodded once, wary.

"And peaceful Sioux camped around Fort Laramie."
No response.

"They've raped white women. And Indian women."
A brief half nod.

"They've killed many men. They've killed some of
the women they . . . tortured first."

Although he remained silent, the sheriff's eyes
were wide and round.

"Some of the women whose breasts they cut off."

"Those were Inj—" The sheriff swallowed his
word. A ripe, red blush crept up his neck all the way
to the surrounded bald spot on the top of his head.

Bane gave no indication he had heard, or could
see, the short, fat man.

"They even killed an entire family, including the
children. A white family. And the little girl . . . they
raped her, too."

The sheriff finally had the grace to look away,
rubbing his chin vigorously.

"And yet you care about the lives of these men.
You do not wish us to kill them, if that is the only way
we can bring them in."

"It ain't that!" the sheriff exclaimed suddenly. "It's
just . . . it's just . . . you—"

"Have a reputation. Yes." Bane rose, elegantly.

247

He placed his palm flat on the notice and looked the sheriff straight in the eye. "Just one more thing."

Blaze watched the man's Adam's apple bob. She finally allowed the smile to creep onto her lips.

"Has anyone ever given you a description of any of these men?"

Blaze could see how intimidated the sheriff was with Bane now towering over him. He appeared a great deal more cooperative and eager to please.

"General . . . uh, just general descriptions, you know. Big men. One has a belly." He attempted a smile that quickly faded. "Dark. Unshaven. Dirty."

"Could be any male in this . . ." Blaze paused to look pointedly out the window, "this ... town."

The sheriff's features melted into an expression of derisive disdain even as he turned in Blaze's direction. Bane slammed his palm down on the desktop. The little man's head nearly swiveled off his neck.

"Did one of them have a scar?"

"A . . . a scar," the sheriff stuttered, voice cracking. "No. No, not that I heard tell."

It was time to leave. Blaze rose, intentionally knocking her chair with the backs of her thighs. She enjoyed watching the sheriff jump when it clattered to the floor. She wheeled and strode toward the door, comforted and buoyed when she heard Bane's familiar step right behind her. Throwing open the door, she walked out into the sunlight of the waning day.

They untied their horses from the hitching rail and swung into the saddles almost simultaneously. It was with grim satisfaction Blaze noticed the stares as they passed along the street, headed out of town. If Bane noticed he gave no sign. He waited until the horses had been walked long enough to limber them up, then kicked his black into a lope. Lonesome was only a step behind, no signal from his rider necessary.

Side by side, they left the town behind.

A blazing sunset caught the rim of the world on fire, bringing sweet closure to the end of a long, but perfect day. Ring plopped down on the front porch steps and hung his arms loosely over his knees. Carrie sat down beside him, her hip just touching his. Normally, he would have glanced her way with a smile. But his gaze remained on the fading colors on the horizon. Nervousness edged into the pit of her stomach.

"Thanks again for all your help today, Ring," Carrie said, testing the temperature of the water that suddenly seemed to have changed.

He looked her way at last. "Thanks for a mighty fine dinner."

"Want me to set the coffee on now?"

"Uh . . ."

As Ring pushed to his feet, Carrie's stomach plummeted. She watched him scrape the stubble on his chin with the heel of his hand.

"What is it, Ring?" she found the courage to ask at last. "What's wrong?"

"Nothing's . . . *wrong*." Ring took his hat off and fingered the brim. He looked off toward the horse corrals. "You got a few nice head. Oughta be able to sell 'em, no problem, when the buyers come around next."

Carrie nodded slowly. "Yeeeeesssss. But they're nice mainly due to you. You have a way with them, Ring."

He shrugged, the gesture pure modesty. His fingers made another trip around his hat brim. Carrie pushed to her feet and walked to his side.

"Ring," she said softly. "I thought we were friends. Please tell me what's wrong . . . what you're thinking."

He seemed all at once to make up his mind.

"Yeah, Carrie, we are friends. That's the problem."

Ring turned on his heel and strode off to the nearest corral, leaning his arms on the top rail. Carrie hurried to join him.

"What on earth do you mean, Ring Crossman?"

He rubbed his chin again, then sighed, long and deeply.

"I got t'get goin', Carrie. It's time to move on. My herd needs t'be in Laramie before the summer gets any older."

It was what she had feared. And it was what she had planned for. Carrie took a deep breath.

"Is that really what you want to do, Ring?"

"Do?" His brows arched, an expression of genuine puzzlement creasing his features. "Horses *are* what I do. What do you mean?"

"There are lots of things you can do with horses, you know."

"Yeah, I know." Ring scratched his head, then pulled his shoulder-length hair back in a fist, as if he was going to tie it in a ponytail. "Buy 'em, trade 'em, train 'em, sell 'em."

Carrie rewarded him with only the faintest of smiles. "You know that's not what I mean."

"It's not?"

He looked so honestly mystified Carrie's smile widened in spite of her best intentions. "Oh, come on, Ring. Don't make me have to do this."

Ring hooked a finger inside his shirt collar and tugged at it, as if it were too tight. "Uh, do what?"

Carrie heaved a sigh of exasperation. "Do you always have to be on the road? Do you always have to move around to sell your horses?"

His lips parted. Carrie could almost see the gears turning in his head.

"We've been doing good work here together on the

farm," she barged on. "We make a good team, Ring. And we're pretty close to Laramie. We could have a major stage depot." High color stained Carrie's cheeks, and her words increased in volume and tempo. "We could sell a lot of horses to the settlers passing through Laramie, not just the stage lines. Other deports, too. We could supply everyone 'round these parts. And, anyway, I've needed the help since . . . since I'm all alone here now." Carrie gave him a moment to let that thought sink in, then hit him with her best shot. "Besides, what if . . . what if the man with the scar—"

Ring grabbed her shoulders so abruptly and firmly it startled her.

"Don't even think it, Carrie. He's a hundred miles from here by now."

"But what if he isn't?" she breathed. An involuntary shiver took her by surprise. She watched the effect of the tremor work its way into Ring's expression. Hope ignited in her breast.

"Are you . . . are you scared, Carrie?"

Scared? Yes. Scared Ring was going to leave.

She nodded. Slowly. With his hands already on her shoulders, it was an easy thing to cup his face in her palms. She stood up on tiptoe and, heart racing, pressed her lips to his.

When she felt his arms slide around her back and his lean, hard body mold to hers, she had a feeling he was considering her idea.

Blaze lay back, head against her saddle, and chewed on a piece of jerky. There could be no fire tonight. Despite the sheriff's reluctance to recognize them as legitimate bounty hunters, they were on the hunt.

"Even if we bring them in," Blaze began, playing the devil's advocate, "the sheriff might refuse us the bounty."

"He won't if we bring them in alive."

"What if we bring them in dead?"

Bane shrugged. "They need killing. But we don't need the bounty." He purposely let his gaze linger on Blaze's saddle. She shifted against it.

"You have a plan, don't you?"

He turned away, silent. But Blaze knew him too well.

In a moment, Bane stooped and picked up a fallen tree branch. He snapped it in half over one knee, then pulled his knife from its sheath and began whittling.

He was good with a knife, Blaze mused. Damn good. But bad with answers. The one she awaited didn't come 'til several long moments later.

"I have a plan," Bane admitted finally.

The tension in his body was so subtle, no one else

would have noticed. Blaze leaned up on one elbow, away from the saddle, and pushed to her feet. Bane continued to whittle.

"Are you going to tell me what it is?"

More minutes ticked away. Bane eventually quit whittling and dropped his hands to his sides. Though she heard no sound, Blaze saw the barely perceptible rise and fall of his shoulders as he drew a long breath and released it.

"It will not be easy."

"None of them ever are."

This time she heard the sigh.

"I know many of the tribes north of here."

It was Blaze's turn to sigh. "And?"

Bane turned to her at last. "I have many friends. They will help us find the men we seek. They will also help us find a herd of buffalo."

"Buffalo?"

Bane dropped abruptly from his feet to a cross-legged position.

"There are six of them, Blaze. Only two of us. We will need help."

"Help . . ."

"I will explain . . ."

The night deepened as Blaze listened, rapt. Disbelieving. At the end she realized her jaw was agape.

"You're . . . you're serious, aren't you?

No response. Not the arch of a brow, the flicker of an eyelid. Blaze turned away and walked to where their animals were tethered. She stroked Lonesome's neck as something clenched tight in her belly. She ran her hands down her mount's shoulder, again and again, until she believed her equilibrium had returned.

It was an amazing plan. Daring. And dangerous. Deadly dangerous.

"It will be hard on the horses," was all she could find to say.

"We will find more horses. We need pack animals as well."

"We'll have to ride back into town. And the sheriff's probably poisoned everyone's mind by now."

"We will not ride back to town. I have heard of a small stage depot . . ."

CHAPTER
TWENTY-SEVEN

RING POUNDED THE LAST NAIL INTO THE TOP RAIL of the corral nearest the house. Shifting the hammer into his left hand, he tested the strength of the board with his right. It held fast. Out of the corner of one eye he caught Carrie looking at him, hands planted on her hips. He twirled the hammer, gunslinger style, and jammed it through his belt. His reward was the melodic sound of her laughter. She joined him at the fence.

"Thanks for doing that, Ring. It's needed doing for a long time."

"Yup. Horses chewed down nearly every one o' them top rails." He turned toward the house and sniffed like a hound testing the air. "What you got cookin'?"

"Stewing chicken, dumplings. Fresh-baked bread."

Ring groaned and pressed a hand to his lean, hard belly. "You tryin' t'spoil me?"

"You betcha."

It was Ring's turn to laugh. "Oh, wait. I know. It's Rowdy's farewell dinner."

"Nope. That's tomorrow night."

Ring turned abruptly serious, and Carrie laid a hand on his arm. He covered it with one of his own, but looked away into the distance, squinting into the red sun setting behind the mountains.

"Ring."

"I'm all right." He patted Carrie's hand. "It's just that we've . . . we've been together a long time."

"I know," she said quietly.

"But he got a good job, with a good outfit." Ring patted Carrie's hand a final time and stepped away, forcing a smile to his lips. "And he'll be back this way."

"In the meantime, you've still got Sandy to raise." The remark drew the desired chuckle.

"Yeah, he's a handful, all right. But a good hand with a horse." He gazed over at the corrals, all of them nearly full. "We need t'get these animals trained up and sold. Feed bill's high, and pens are overcrowded."

"We have an order for four already, don't forget, and more customers inquiring almost every day."

Ring didn't miss the note of pride in Carrie's voice. He had to concede her idea had been a good one, and for more than one reason.

He was tired of the endless wandering, he had to

admit, and he liked the training side of the business better anyway. Time to let someone else go out and find the horses. It was more than okay with Sandy, too, it seemed. His leg still bothered him some, and long hours in the saddle on the trail weren't doing him, or it, any good. Ring pushed back his hat and pulled at his chin. Yep, it had been the right decision. And the best part of it was standing right next to him.

Carrie had remained silent and immobile, instinctively knowing Ring was mentally weighing his decision. She didn't realize she'd been holding her breath until he exhaled a long sigh and put his hands on her shoulders. Her heart raced, then melted, when she looked into his eyes.

It had been devastating losing her parents. If it hadn't been for Ring, she didn't know what she would have done. At first she had simply been grateful for his helpfulness, his kindness, and the gentle nature of his spirit. She wasn't sure when gratitude had turned into love, and she didn't care. She only knew she wanted to care for this good man until the end of her days.

Ring could read the yearning in her expression, in the very lines and angles of her body. He wondered briefly what he'd done to earn such a reward at the end of his long, hard trail, then decided it didn't matter, not one damn bit. Somewhere along the way he must have done something good. And it sure was all good now. As he leaned toward her, he watched her eyes close and parted his lips in anticipation of hers.

The sound of hoofbeats startled them both, and they moved away from each other. Ring swore softly under his breath and edged backward toward his rifle sheath slung over a fence post.

"There's two of them," Carrie said.

"I see that." Ring eased the rifle out of its sheath.

The dust cloud drew nearer, but it was hard to make out the riders in the failing light of dusk. Ring let the rifle hang at his side, barrel pointed at the ground. The riders weren't coming at a hard gallop, but a leisurely lope.

"Ring?" Carrie took a tentative step forward. "You know the horse you gave me, the pelouse, Gus?"

Ring only nodded in response, and Carrie turned to look at him. "Yes," he said aloud, and she returned her attention to the oncoming riders.

"I swear one that's coming looks just like him," she said softly.

Her younger eyes had spotted it first, but Ring finally made it out himself. The markings were distinctive. It surely was one of the Nez Perce horses. The hair on his forearms stood up.

It couldn't be.

Slowly, deliberately, Ring put his rifle back in its sheath. Carrie looked at him levelly.

"You know them. Don't you?"

Ring nodded, but Carrie felt no great sense of relief. Something was wrong. She turned back toward the riders and studied them.

Both wore buckskins. Both had long, black hair, but one was clearly a woman. The one riding the spotted horse. Something unpleasant fluttered in Carrie's belly.

The riders reined their mounts to a jog and approached more slowly, nonthreateningly. The man raised his hand in a gesture that was part greeting, part indication he intended no harm. Carrie was surprised to note that although he appeared to be of Indian blood, his eyes were as blue as a morning sky. Her gaze flicked to the woman.

Her beauty was as striking as the blaze of white in her ebon hair. The uncomfortable feeling in Carrie's stomach crept up closer to her heart. The woman's eyes widened, her lips parted, and her gaze riveted on Ring. Carrie looked over her shoulder.

The expression on his face was unfathomable. He took off his hat and held it against his chest.

"I'll be damned," Ring said in a voice so low Carrie barely heard it. "I'll be damned."

The man and woman dismounted and exchanged glances. Then the woman walked forward. Ring moved to meet her. Three paces apart, they halted.

Carrie watched a tear slip from the woman's eye.

Saw her raise her arms. Looked on in disbelief as her man moved into the woman's embrace.

Profound silence followed Blaze's disclosure. Ring resisted the immediate impulse to look at Carrie. He did not want Blaze, or Bane, to misinterpret what they might see in his expression. He did not want them to think he condemned them in any way. But Carrie, pushing abruptly away from the rough-hewn kitchen table, spoke aloud the words swirling in his head.

"You're the ones we've been hearing about! You're the bounty hunters . . . and you *know* Ring!"

Carrie was on her feet in an instant, and clapped both hands over her mouth. Bane rose with slow dignity from the table.

"Thank you for your kind invitation to stay for dinner, but we have to be moving on. If you'd still sell us the horses, we'd be grateful."

Ring didn't move except to look up at Bane, then at Carrie.

"People gotta do what they gotta do," he said evenly. "Sit back down, Bane. You're still welcome to stay for dinner. Carrie, this woman here, who calls herself Blaze, got that name from me. And I gave it to her when she saved Sandy's life."

Carrie's hands fell away from her face. She felt her jaw drop. Everything was happening a little too fast, and now it was a little too overwhelming. Unusual strangers had ridden into her place, Ring apparently knew them, he had an emotional moment with the woman, invited them into her house, she learned they were the infamous bounty-hunting couple, and now . . .

"Sit down, Carrie honey, before you fall down," Ring urged gently and pulled back her chair.

"No, we should leave." Blaze rose and moved to Bane's side. "We never should have come into your home in the first place." Together they turned to leave.

"No, wait!" Carrie hurried to the door and stood in front of it. "I'm so sorry. I didn't mean to sound rude. I just . . . I was just so surprised . . ."

Ring finally pushed to his feet and joined Carrie by the door, putting a comforting arm around her shoulders. He looked Bane straight in the eye.

"Please stay," he said simply. "You're my friends. Nothing can ever change that." Ring dared at last to look at Blaze, and he knew she comprehended his sincerity.

The moment came to an abrupt end when the sound of hissing and spitting came from the wood-stove top.

"Oh my gosh. My stew!"

Blaze welcomed the interruption. It not only ended the awkward moment, but gave her the chance to do what she knew she must. For Ring.

"I'll help Carrie clean up and get dinner on the table."

He got the message.

"Why don't you and I go look at those horses," he said to Bane.

Bane nodded and followed Ring outside. Grabbing a towel, Blaze lifted the heavy stew pot off the stove.

"You don't have to do that!" Carrie protested. "I—"

"You've made Ring happy," Blaze cut in. "I prayed he would find someone. He's a good man."

Carrie dropped her chin to her chest as color flooded her cheeks, completely at a loss for words.

"He says I saved Sandy's life," Blaze continued gently. "But Ring saved mine as well. Without him I wouldn't be standing here speaking to you."

Carrie forced herself to meet Blaze's dark gaze. Curiosity burned like a hot iron.

"He . . . he said he gave you your name. Blaze."

"Yes." Blaze steeled herself. It would be good to tell Ring's woman the story, good to have its fire in her blood. She inclined her head at the table. Carrie accepted the wordless invitation and sat, hands folded in her lap, and Blaze sat across from her.

"He gave me that name because I would not tell him the name my parents gave me when I was born," she began, voice low and controlled. "I left that name behind when I buried all the people of my village and all my family, my mother and father and brother, Tomas. Evil men wanted black-haired scalps; they turn them in to the government for bounty, saying they are Apache."

This time when Carrie raised her hands to her mouth it was to stem the nausea.

"They killed my people and took their scalps. They left me for dead." Blaze touched the white streak in her hair. "I buried them all. Every one. At the end of three days I was done. I took off my clothes—clothes stiff with blood—and walked into the mountains. I began a new life."

Without even realizing what she was doing, Carrie took one hand from her face and reached across the table. Blaze let her take her hand, although she did not return the pressure of her fingers.

"I taught myself how to shoot," she went on, "and I started hunting evil men. I earned enough to stay alive. I only needed to learn to ride a horse so I could pursue the most evil men of all. That's when Ring found me."

Blaze recounted her time with Ring in the mountains, and Sandy's healing. She told of the journey to Phoenix, the horse, and Ring's mother. When she saw tears well in Carrie's eyes, the numbness seemed to leave her fingers and she squeezed the girl's hand. She finished her tale with the day she and Bane said good-bye to Ring.

"I have not seen him since, until today. You know of my life with Bane since that day, you have heard. And now I know of Ring's. I have seen."

Blaze permitted the smile that came to her lips from her heart, and Carrie returned it, intuitively understanding, and cherishing, all it implied.

"I . . . I apologize again for my . . . my reaction when I realized who you were. I didn't mean to judge you. I'm so very sorry for the terrible things that happened to you, and I . . . I understand why you do . . . what you do."

"And why we will continue," Bane said.

Both women looked up, startled. Engrossed in their conversation, neither had heard the men reenter.

"Blaze," Bane said, his voice cold and hard. "Ring has told me about his woman." He glanced briefly at Carrie. "Her parents were killed, her mother raped first." His eyes came back to Carrie. "Tell her. Tell Blaze of the man you saw," he commanded.

Carrie sat erect, pushing her spine into the back of the chair for support. Her fingers trailed across the table, away from Blaze's hand. With visible effort, eyes tightly shut, she forced herself to speak.

"I'll never forget him," she whispered, and raised a hand to her cheek. "He had a scar . . . here. A scar like lightning."

When she opened her eyes at last, it was to see the woman's face across from her was bloodless.

CHAPTER TWENTY-EIGHT

DEEP NIGHT BLANKETED THE NORTHERN PLAINS. Clouds dimmed the stars, and the intermittent light of the half moon did little to relieve the darkness. It did not help Blaze sleep. She lay still and listened to the small sounds of the night that existed within the small copse of trees where they had made camp. There were rustlings in the sparse undergrowth and in the branches over their heads. The nearby stream, an off-shoot of the Bighorn River, burbled noisily. When she heard a distant howling, Blaze wondered idly if it was a coyote or a wolf. Bane would know.

And then, as if she had conjured him, he was at her side.

"You cannot sleep."

"No."

"Do you fear the morrow?"

"I fear nothing when I'm with you," she replied honestly.

Bane lowered himself to the ground and stretched out beside her.

"You have been . . . quiet . . . in the days since we saw your friend and his woman."

"I've never been talkative, Bane." Blaze smiled in the darkness. "You know that. And they're your friends, too."

He nodded slowly, thoughtfully. "Yes. They are friends to us both. And not only because we now share a common purpose."

Blaze held her tongue, remembering the painful scene following Carrie's revelation. The circumstances had forced her to retell, and relive, her brother's hanging. Bane had had to add his own part of the story. Carrie's shock and horror had been difficult to watch. And Ring had grieved for them all.

The scarred man. Jake. The author of so much pain, so much sorrow, so much destruction. The terrible irony of the coincidence was not lost on her either. But it had brought them all together, and that was a good thing. In the midst of a scarred landscape, a single flower bloomed.

"Ring is pretty sure we're headed in the right direction, isn't he?" Blaze said at length.

"He said when they lost the trail it was headed

north. Yes."

"And you believe we'll find him somewhere near Fort Laramie."

"Yes."

They listened to the night sounds together for awhile. Blaze lay on her back with her hands clasped at her waist. She was surprised when Bane's hand covered hers.

"I must make a confession to you."

Blaze turned her head in Bane's direction, brows arched in amazement, lips forming a perfect O. She saw amusement reflected in his eyes. And something else.

"Ring cared for you, as he now feels for Carrie. Yet you did not return the affection."

"I did, Bane. But only as a friend."

"Because your feelings were for me."

The silence stretched. "Yes, that's true," Blaze said at last.

"And I have love for you as well. You know this."

She could only nod. A strange stricture had formed in her throat.

"After the bear's attack, I did not think it wise to allow that part of our . . . relationship to continue. Our lives, our goal, depended on our focus, our total commitment to our purpose. I believed this. I do not believe it any longer. I was wrong."

"Bane—"

"So much bad, so much evil has come from the man who raped my mother. But now there is good as well," he went on, as if he had read her earlier thoughts. "There is friendship, and united purpose, and the love Ring has found for this woman. These things are good. They are reasons to stay alive. And to celebrate life."

It was the longest, most profound speech Blaze had ever heard him make. Her heart twisted, and her gut wrenched. She wanted to tell him what was in her heart, how much he mattered to her, how much she loved him.

"Bane," she tried again.

This time his finger touched her lips, stilling her voice. His mouth followed.

The kiss was slow at first, deep, as they rediscovered each other's taste and texture. Blaze wondered if Bane could taste the tears in her throat. She threaded her fingers through his hair and held him to her as if she feared he might draw away, only letting go to help him pull the buckskin shirt up and off.

Then his lips were in the valley between her breasts. Cupping them in his palms and massaging the nipples to erectness, he moved lower, trailing kisses down to her navel. When he nuzzled the junction of her thighs through the tight buckskin pants, Blaze thought she might lose her mind with the overload of sensation.

Groaning, she pulled him back up on top of her so his hardness pressed there instead, and rocked against him in a near frenzy.

She helped him remove his own buckskins, nearly tearing them from the body she wanted, needed to touch, the flesh she needed to feel against hers. And when finally they both were naked, she wrapped her legs around him and pulled him atop her once more.

It had been too long. The repressed yearning was too great. Deliberately positioning herself, opening her legs, she thrust upward and let him fill her to the hilt. For a long moment she savored the feel of him, the hard, thick length of him throbbing ever so faintly within her, and then could wait no longer.

It didn't take long. Blaze exploded after only a few brief thrusts, and soon watched Bane grimace with the intensity of his own release. Panting, he collapsed on her chest. But she gave him only minutes.

The far-off howl repeated, and Blaze began moving her hips again to the music of the night.
And this time, the dance was not swiftly over.

CHAPTER
TWENTY-NINE

IT WAS A PERFECT MOMENT. THERE WERE FEW, SO few in her life. Blaze drew inside herself to savor it.

They lay side by side, touching, side molded to side. Their hands were clasped, warm between her right thigh and his left. Though dawn had broken, the sky was dim, clouded. She heard the sound of raindrops hitting the leafy canopy that sheltered them. A single drop plopped on her eyebrow, then ran into her eye like a tear. Beside her, Bane took a deep breath.

The moment was almost over. She wondered when another might come again. Perhaps never. They were bounty hunters. They had no home; maybe not even a future.

Blaze hugged the moment tighter. Would she change anything? A glimpse of Ring's mother's cozy house flickered across the back of her eyelids. But the answer was

272

no. Her fingers tightened around Bane's hand, and she felt him return the squeeze. Her heart spasmed.

For good or evil, whether they continued their life or found death, she was where she was meant to be. Bane's words of the previous evening returned to wrap their warmth around her soul.

They had begun with one purpose. They had become one heart.

Blaze suppressed her regret when Bane rolled away from her. The rain was falling in earnest. Distant thunder rolled across the plains, and the horses stirred nervously. She moved into a crouch, then rose.

Bane saddled their mounts, removed the hobbles from the pack horses, and loosely haltered them, tying the lead ropes to the packs. They would follow without urging.

Blaze climbed into her saddle wordlessly. The peace of the morning slipped away despite her desperate attempt to hold on to it. Bane loved her. He had spoken the words sacred to her heart. He was her love, her life. And now they were on the way to their most difficult, dangerous mission yet. Blaze put her heels to Lonesome's sides.

Their horses jogged, side by side, through the long, sere grass. The plains were a virtual sea of grass, the mountains silent, watchful leviathans. A distant stand of cottonwood trees marked the course of a river.

They were alone in the vastness.

And then, suddenly, they were alone no longer.

The mounted braves moved up on them from behind, flanking them. Lonesome and the black mare moved into an easy lope to match pace with the other horses. Bane looked neither right nor left, and Blaze followed his lead.

The ground eventually became more hilly; they had reached the mountains' foothills. Cresting a rise, they reined to a halt. All eyes were on a growing dust cloud.

"You see," one of the braves said at last, "we did not fail you."

"I knew you would not," Bane replied.

"They will be coming soon. You have not much time." The brave swiveled on his horse and pointed. "There is a canyon. There. The camp is just beyond the first bend."

"You have my gratitude."

"We have done what we can. We can do no more. These men have cost us too much already. And your plan is a dangerous one."

Bane remained silent. Then: "Again, I thank you."

Holding his black mare to a walk, they descended, loose rocks skittering around them. At the bottom Bane urged his horse back to a canter, then a gallop. Blaze became acutely aware of the time and the first twinge of nervousness clutched at her belly. Bane had mentioned he knew many tribes in this area; had many friends. His plan was coming together. They were on their way.

The dust cloud obliterating the horizon to the east was coming inexorably closer. On flat ground, the horses stretched out into the run, manes and tails streaming. They headed for the mouth of the canyon and rode right in when they reached it. Bane glanced once over his shoulder, eyes measuring, assessing the growing, advancing cloud. With a nod of his head he signaled her to ride on.

Exactly as the braves had described to them, the elaborate camp, set amid some brushy growth, was right in the center of the wide, dry riverbed not too far back. At the sound of pounding hoofbeats, the motley band of men had gathered into a rough circle in front of their tents. Six hands reached for six holstered pistols. It was Blaze's cue.

"There are too many!" she shrieked. "Go back! Go back!"

Yanking on the reins, Blaze wheeled Lonesome to the right. Glancing over her left shoulder she saw Bane do the same. The outlaws were just mounting their own horses, pistols drawn.

Their lead was slim. Blaze leaned low over Lonesome's neck and heard a shot whistle past her ear.

From the corner of her eye she could see Bane literally hanging on the black mare's side, making the smallest target possible.

They weren't far from the mouth of the canyon, and burst out onto the plain at a dead run. The buffalo herd was exactly where Bane had planned for it to be. His friends had executed their part of the plan expertly.

Blaze could smell them, rank and musky, the stink mingled with dust. Their hooves beat a deadly rhythm on the dry ground. She swiveled her head and saw the gang was still following. Because of the pounding of their own horses' hooves, they had apparently not heard the buffalo thunder. And, focused on the Indian and his squaw, they also had not noticed the dust cloud.

They finally saw the herd, but too late. Blaze watched them try to turn their horses, but the animals were panicked and uncontrollable.

Riding calmly at the edge of the herd, going along with the direction of the stampeding bison, both Bane and Blaze calmly raised their guns.

She'd brought down men without a moment of hesitation or a pang of remorse. But this was different. Blaze took a deep breath and gently squeezed the trigger. Her shot rang out, swiftly followed by another. Two horses went down swiftly and silently. Then it was their riders.

Four more shots; six dead horses. The herd took care of the remainder of the riders.

The stampede was fading thunder. Lonesome and the black mare stood with heads low, breathing heavily, sides lathered and dripping. Blaze loosened their girths and removed the saddles and blankets. Cupping her hands, she ran them over the horses' slick and glistening sides, removing as much sweat as possible. Then she walked them in slow circles.

Bane noted her care of their animals, but remained fixed on his grisly task. Soothing the nervous pack horse with his left hand, he tightened the ropes holding the body to the pack frame with his right. The smell of death assailed his nostrils, the same stench that spooked the pack animal.

All six pack horses were laden in short order with the help of the braves. Then they sat atop their own mounts admiring the loot they had recently acquired: guns, holsters, belts, and boots. Even one sweat-stained Stetson. The brave jammed it on his head to the immediate and loud delight of his companions. Snorting derisively they pointed at him and laughed. In response he tossed the hat in the hair and emptied his new revolver into it.

Blaze tacked Lonesome and the mare and took the three lead ropes Bane handed up to her. He swung a long leg over the mare and sat tall and straight in his saddle.

"Again, my thanks, my brothers," he said.

"If you need our help again, you know where we will be."

Bane nodded. "I do need your help again."

All eyes were riveted on Bane, Blaze's included. A funny buzz of premonition vibrated up her spine.

"Ask," one of the braves said.

"I need your eyes. To know what you have seen."

"Ask," the brave repeated.

"We are on the trail of a bad man," Bane replied briskly. He lifted a finger to his cheek. "He has a scar, here. We have heard he was around Fort Laramie."

"You heard right."

Only by tremendous exercise of control did Blaze manage to swallow her cry. Bane's expression remained immobile and impassive. She couldn't imagine how he did it.

The brave who had spoken leaned over and spit. "The scarred man bought a squaw from a hunter just down from the mountains."

Blaze repressed a shudder.

"Do you know where he is now?" Bane asked stonily.

"It is said he went up into the mountains to trap."

"He took the squaw to the mountains to hide his torture from her people," another said. Then he, too, spit.

"Why do you think this?" Bane demanded.

But the braves remained silent. Sensing the tension in the air, the horses shuffled nervously.

"As you told," one of the braves finally said, "he is a bad man. But his fate, I think, has hunted him down."

"Aye," Bane hissed under his breath. "The storm has come . . ."

CHAPTER THIRTY

"Never seen any damn thing like this." Grimacing, the sheriff cut the last rope binding the body to the pack frame. The heavy-bellied corpse dropped to the ground with a sickening thud, and the sheriff stepped back. He pulled a dirty bandana from a back pocket and shoved it under his nose.

"Six," Bane said into the silence. He glanced at the other five bloodied bodies, similarly and unceremoniously strewn on the ground.

"I kin count," the sheriff grunted belatedly. He kicked at the closest body with the toe of his boot. "What'chou do to 'em?"

"Ended their reign of terror," Bane replied brusquely.

"How'd ya do it? Knock a mountain over on 'em?"

"A mountain of flesh, yes," Bane said with a chuckle in his voice only Blaze heard.

The sheriff screwed up his forehead with puzzlement. "Thought you was gonna try to bring 'em in alive this time."

"We were outnumbered," Bane said evenly. "As you see. We did what we had to do."

The sheriff made a rude noise. "Get some help 'n get 'em over to the doc's," he said to someone over his shoulder. The lean, acne-scarred kid looked like he wished he could be anywhere else on earth. "But . . . but . . . Sheriff," he stuttered. "They're already—"

"I *know* that, moron. Just do as I say!"

Blaze lightly touched the tips of Bane's fingers, and he turned in her direction. By mute agreement they walked toward their horses tied to the hitching rail in front of the jail.

The sheriff stuck a cheroot in his mouth, bit the end off and spit it out. "Don't tell me yer leavin' already. Ain'tcha gonna worry me over the bounty?"

"Don't want it; don't need it." Bane pulled his reins out of the slip knot and mounted. "Just hand me the leads to my pack animals."

Blaze had all she could do to keep from laughing. The danger they had faced, the horror of what they had done, melted away, and she felt a weight drop from her shoulders as she threw her leg over Lonesome's back. Bane, usually the most serious of men, had turned their previous situation with the sheriff completely around. She had not missed the chuckle in his voice or the twinkle in his eye.

It was a day well ended. They had won. On many levels. And the greatest victory of all was almost within their grasp.

They were an hour south of town before Bane answered Blaze's unvoiced question.

"We will return the pack horses. We won't need them where we're going."

There. He'd said it. It was out. Soon they would be on their way. A shiver passed through Blaze's entire body.

Ring and Carrie stood shoulder to shoulder in the fading light, hands lightly touching the top rail of one of the pens.

"The horses are none the worse for wear," Ring said in the same tone he used to gentle a frightened animal.

Carrie stepped back, waving a hand in front of her nose. "As soon as the stink wears off they'll be fine." She tried to smile but the effort failed. She jerked her head toward the house. "The horses aren't the ones I'm worried about anyway."

Mere tone of voice wasn't going to work this time. Ring didn't know what to say. He was worried, too.

Removing his hands from the rail, he hooked his index fingers into his back pockets and took a deep breath.

Carrie knew tipping the hat back would be next. She didn't have to wait long.

"Shall we check on 'em?" Ring cleared his throat.

A splash of water on dry ground temporarily stayed Carrie's words. "Guess that's our answer. Bath time's over."

It was an amazing feeling to be clean. It was even more incredible to be standing in Carrie's home, a home she apparently now shared with Ring. Ring . . .

Blaze's eyes unfocused as her mind drifted back to the past. She was only dimly aware of Bane shrugging into his spare, clean buckskin shirt. Ring. How long ago it seemed she had met him in her wild mountain home. That time had been the beginning of her second life. The first was so far in the past she feared it might have become inaccessible. But it had not.

Warmth accompanied the initial recollection of her family. Then the horror washed over her, the grief and pain. She balled her fists and dug her ragged nails into her palms. Her spine stiffened as the heat of revenge coursed through her veins, drying her tears before they could fall.

"Blaze?"

She turned to Bane and saw the question in his eyes. Their connection was nearly palpable.

"I'm all right. I'll be better when we . . ."

Bane nodded. "Let's ride."

It was as difficult saying good-bye again to Ring as it was the time she had left him at the camp and ridden off with Bane, and for the same reason. She knew she might never see him again. The only difference was that this time the prize was almost within their grasp. And the chances greater they would never meet again.

Knowing now what she did about the beautiful Mexican girl and the half-breed Apache who was, obviously, more than simply a partner in their quest for vengeance, there was no jealousy in her heart when she watched Ring and Blaze embrace in what might be a final farewell. In fact, she had to swipe the tears from her cheeks. Choking back a sob, she watched Ring and Bane clasp hands.

"Hey, honey." This time it was Ring whose long, calloused fingers brushed the emotional rain from her freckled cheekbones.

"Oh, Ring," she sighed and wrapped her arms around his waist as the riders disappeared into their own dust cloud. "What if they—"

"But they won't," Ring finished for her. "I kin feel

it in m'bones. They're special people, an' there's somethin' special atween 'em. Like . . ."

It was Carrie's turn to finish a thought, and she did it with her lips.

"Yeah," Ring agreed. "Just like that."

He had thought the matter was settled, but tears returned to well in her eyes. "What's wrong now, little honey?"

Carrie rubbed her nose with the back of one hand. "I . . . I feel partly responsible for . . . for what they're doing. If something happens to them—"

"Stop. Nothin's gonna happen, number one. Number two, they have to do it anyway. You know that."

"Yeah, I guess I do," she conceded. "But—"

"No 'buts' but this one." Ring smoothed his hands down from Carrie's waist and felt her respond by leaning into him and feeling the growing evidence of his affection for her. Maybe this was exactly what they both needed at this particular moment.

Despite his reassuring words to Carrie, Ring wasn't so all-fired sure in his heart things were going to work out right either. The man they were about to tree was a monster, a sick bastard.

The last thing Ring saw when he closed his eyes and lowered his lips to Carrie's was the streak of white in Blaze's black hair.

The story of how it got there was still a mystery to

him. Blaze had to come back. She owed him the tale.

The thought wasn't as comforting as he had hoped it would be, and he swooped Carrie into his arms. Time to make the world go away.

CHAPTER THIRTY-ONE

A PIECE OF GREEN STICK FINALLY CAUGHT FIRE FROM one its drier neighbors within the ring of stone, and the flame flared to life with a hiss and a curl of dark, acrid smoke. Jake, leaning forward to catch the campfire's warmth as night stole the heat of the day, thrust his scarred visage directly into smoke. Rubbing his eyes angrily with the backs of his fists, he spat.

"What the hell's matter with you, squaw, putting green wood in the fire?"

Knowing what was likely to come next, the woman cringed away from the burly figure sitting across from her, but to no avail. Despite his bulk, he was quick. And brutal.

Only when the squaw's knees buckled and her eyes started to roll up in her head did Jake loosen his grip on her throat. There were still things he needed from her.

He let her drop to the ground and administered a kick in the gut for good measure. An involuntary grunt escaped her, and he smiled in satisfaction. Damn Injuns never liked to give anything away, especially a reaction to pain.

Raven's Wing, as she had been known to her husband and family, remained curled in a fetal position until she could breathe normally again, then sat up slowly. She eyed the scarred man warily.

The trapper who had first stolen her had been a bad man, but not as bad as this one. This man was evil. She narrowed her eyes.

The fire burned low, and night closed in on them tightly. She knew he could not see her, but she knew he could hear. And she knew something else. It gave her the strength she sought from deep within.

"Be afraid, bad man."

Jake snorted his disgust. How dare the woman speak to him at all, much less issue such a warning?

"Be afraid," she continued, "because you are a bad man and the Punishers can see you."

Jake spat into the dying flames again, taking no pleasure from the angry hiss it spat back at him. He was about to tell the squaw bitch to shut the hell up when she repeated her strange words.

"Be afraid, bad man, because the Punishers have eagle eyes and magical powers and can see you through the darkness."

Hating the fear that churned in his bowels, he tried to steel himself against the chill that crawled up his spine, but he was helpless in its grip. No doubt about it, Injun women were witchy, and the squaw's words iced his blood. He remembered another woman long, long ago and touched the jagged scar on his face.

She'd been a pretty one, slim but busty. He'd caught her working alone, hoeing something in a planted field, and he did what a man had to do. She'd fought back, hell yes, she had fought. She was a rare one, beautiful and strong, and as she clawed at him and screamed, she screamed a curse at him in his own language. She spoke the white man's language, and he had been overcome with rage. How could she have known his language, *his* language? She was less than an animal. It wasn't right.

He had strangled her until he thought she was dead. But she wasn't, and she screamed the curse again as her nails dug into his face and tore a jagged hole down his face.

"You are marked by the lightning . . . lightning will take you!"

Raven's Wing smelled the white man's fear. She could almost feel it, a wall of dark emotion coming at her through the night. She sniffed like a wolf scenting the wind, and held the other thing she knew close to her breast to keep it warm.

The Punishers were out there. She had heard them, the small sounds they made as they hid and watched; sounds the scarred man could not hear with his white man's ears. They were hunters, but it was not game they hunted; it was the scarred man.

It made her wonder if some of her people had come for her, because whoever watched was wise to the ways of the ground, and trees, and wind. It made her smile in the darkness.

The trickster coyote must have put the thought in her head to call them the Punishers and frighten the scarred man. Yet she knew they were here to punish him. Why else did they hunt him? And he was, as she had accused him, a bad man. He must have harmed others; it was his nature.

Now fate had come for him. Raven's Wing picked up a stick and poked at the fire. In response it flared back to life.

Good. Maybe they could see him better. Maybe they would strike tonight. She hoped so, prayed so. She did not want to feel his hands reaching for her again.

The Great Spirit was with them. He had delivered His word through the mouth of the Sioux woman.

The lightning would, indeed, take the devil who had fathered him. He reached out and stroked the white streak in Blaze's hair. But what about the thunder? Bane's fists clenched involuntarily.

Then he noticed the darkening of the night. It began at the corners of his vision. The periphery faded, and objects directly in front of him began to lose definition. He blinked and raised his gaze skyward.

The moon was obscured. Even as he watched the stars winked out, seemingly one by one. He sniffed the air.

Rain clouds. An uncharacteristic chill trembled through his limbs. Head still lifted, he scented the wind once again.

It was coming soon. Under its cover they would put his plan in motion; the plan the wise woman had sent him from the Great Spirit.

Although they did not touch, Blaze could feel his tension. She also smelled the coming rain. Intuitively, she knew Bane would use it to aid them.

Moments later the first fat drops fell on the leaves of the tree beneath which they sheltered. Blaze ran a hand lightly over her hair and felt the moisture, then waited for the signal she knew would come from the man at her side. The irony of the moment—the weather—did not escape her.

Bane waited patiently until the rain fell in earnest.

The downpour hitting foliage and pummeling the ground would cover all sounds of their approach. With the slightest nod of his head, he motioned Blaze to follow him.

Blaze tightened Lonesome's cinch and climbed into the wet saddle, soaking the only part of her clothing still dry. Her horse fell in behind Bane's as the mare picked her way carefully down the mountain slope. Having scouted the camp earlier, they would have no trouble finding it again, even in the driving rain.

CHAPTER THIRTY-TWO

THE SIOUX WOMAN HEARD THEM COMING, DESPITE the overlaying sound of the rain, and knew the scarred man had not. The only thing he had heard were the sounds she had made on behalf of the Punishers. Smiling to herself, she kept her head bowed, giving nothing away, as she packed her captor's few belongings and secured them to the back of his saddle. Steeped in the comforting memory of the fear she had caused the scarred man, she did not hear him creep up behind her.

"Git out the way, squaw!"

She moved away from the horse, but not fast enough. He roughly grabbed her shoulder and spun her in the opposite direction, then punched her between the shoulder blades. The air whooshed out of her lungs, and she fell to her knees, sodden hair brushing the ground.

A grin wrinkled Jake's scar. He felt a stirring in his loins and drew back his right leg.

Raven's Wing heard her rib crack. Pain was a live thing eating into her core, devouring flesh and muscle and bone. She could no longer breathe. Blessedly semiconscious, she was barely aware when the scarred man kicked her on the other side.

The silent communication between Blaze and Bane was eloquent. The woman must not die. It was time.

The plan was to simply ride down on him. Mounted or unmounted, he would be no match for the two of them. They would probably even have the Sioux woman's help. They would overpower him, tie him to his horse, and deliver his stinking hide to the sheriff.

Blaze regretted they had not moved sooner. Her consolation was that the woman would never again suffer his brutalities.

Bane made no signal, just put his heels to the black mare, and both horses barreled down the lower slope of the mountain at full gallop. There was no longer any need for stealth. Under cover of the storm, they had moved in as close as they needed to be. There was no way their prey could elude them now.

Blaze sat as far back in the saddle as she could and gave Lonesome his head. Squatting nearly to his haunches, front legs alternately bracing and moving forward, they sent a rain of rocks and dirt in front of them as they scrambled down the slope.

The black mare was slightly ahead when they reached the bottom. Hearing the commotion, Jake had looked up in alarm, turned, and run for his horse. The Sioux woman lay still.

Out of control, slipping and sliding as she neared the bottom, the black mare was off balance. Trying to help her regain her footing by remaining perfectly still in the center of his saddle cost Bane precious moments. Jake gained his horse and cruelly put his spurs into its ribs. With a squeal the animal leapt away. Bane was directly behind him, with Blaze in hot pursuit of them both. Glancing over her shoulder, she saw the Indian woman hobbling along in a semicrouch.

Blaze saw him lean in his saddle and knew exactly what he was going to do. He had told her in the deep of the night.

"It will be easy to take him," Bane had whispered under the sound of the wind, breath blowing softly on her neck. "We will use stealth and strike quickly."

Blaze had no doubt Bane could overpower Jake even though the scarred man was much larger. Yet she was not completely at ease with the plan. "What if he gets to his horse?"

"We will run him down. No horse is swifter than my black. I will take him from his saddle like the mountain lion takes the pronghorn. Then we will bind him and deliver him to his fate."

No mention of weapons was made. Blaze knew they had to bring him back alive. Not because of the reward, but because Jake was Bane's father. And Bane wanted to watch him dangle at the end of a rope. Blaze rubbed her neck reflexively. A bullet was too swift, too painless. Jake had to pay. Jake *would* pay. For all of them.

As Bane had boldly predicted, he took their quarry like a lion pulled down the antelope. Taking a moment to calculate distance and force, Bane coiled and, an instant later, sprang.

"*Oof.*" Jake grunted loudly when Bane made violent contact with his body. Nearly toppled from the saddle, he saved himself by grasping the pommel with both hands, one on top of the other.

Jake rooted to the saddle, momentum gone, Bane could not dislodge his quarry. Hanging on to the meaty form with his left arm around his waist, Bane drew back his right arm and aimed a punch at Jake's right temple. He connected with a sickening *thud*.

Jake swayed, but did not go down. Blaze knew her moment had come. She knew it in her mind and in her body; in the heat that rose from the pit of her belly and coursed through her limbs, driving her.

Lonesome remained steady when Blaze launched herself from the saddle, staying near the black mare as they ran.

It all went wrong in the blink of an eye. Jake's horse, thrown off balance and laboring under the additional weight, stumbled and went to its knees.

"Blaze!"

She felt him clutch at her, grabbing a handful of buckskin, and then they were rolling over the wet ground. As had been his intention, they were well away from the fallen horse, thrashing as it attempted to regain its feet. The black and Lonesome ran on while Bane and Blaze scrambled on hands and knees in Jake's direction.

"Git away! Git away, dammit!" Jake howled, kicking with one leg at his still-struggling horse to induce it to get up, using the other to send a spray of rocks and damp sand in the direction of his pursuers.

Bane's knife appeared in his hand. Blaze's fingers gripped her pistol.

Bane reached him first and hauled him to his feet, cursing and grunting. Blaze leveled her gun.

"No, Blaze." Bane had one of Jake's arms twisted painfully behind his back. His knife was pressed to the man's throat. "Get my hobbles."

Their horses were just disappearing in a cloud of dust. Blaze put her fingers to lips and whistled. Lonesome turned around at once, the mare following.

In the meantime, Bane had wrestled Jake to the

ground and had him facedown, eating mud, a knee in his kidneys and the knife still at his throat. Blaze's left hand fisted, and the right had a death grip on the gun. The urge to kill rose in Blaze so powerfully it nearly choked her. Only a nudge from her horse distracted her from the object of her obsession.

"Blaze . . . the hobbles."

Fingers numb and fumbling, Blaze untied the latigo on the front left side of her saddle, freeing the leather-braided hobbles. She brought them to Bane and knelt at his side.

"Take the knife," he ordered curtly.

Blaze didn't hesitate. Braving the man's stink, she leaned in and took the knife from Bane's fingers. She couldn't resist pressing the blade into the reeking, sweaty flesh. The man howled.

"Don't kill me! What'd I do?"

Silently, Bane secured Jake's hands with the hobbles, then grabbed a handful of sodden, greasy hair and pulled his head back. Blaze had to move quickly to keep the knife in position.

The Sioux woman had finally caught up with them. She knelt to one side, long, wet hair hanging on either side of her pinched face. Blaze knew she was in pain. But the ghost of a smile flitted across the woman's lips when Bane thrust his face into Jake's and bared his teeth.

"What did you do?" he hissed. With a brutal twist of his wrist, he turned Jake's head toward Blaze. The rain, which had faded to a drizzle, suddenly seemed to renew its strength. A crack of thunder made Jake cringe.

"Look at her!" Bane gave Jake a shake. "Look at her and know what you did."

Blaze touched the streak of white in her hair.

Jake tried to shake his head in bewildered denial, but Bane held him steady.

"You shot her. See the path of your bullet? You killed every person in her village and you hanged her brother."

"You're crazy, Injun!" Jake spat, and a gob of saliva landed on Bane's cheek. He let the rain wash it away.

"And you're a murderer," Bane said quietly. "A murderer and a rapist." His grip on Jake's hair tightened, and he pulled the man's head back farther.

"*Gaaaack.*"

"Is that all you've got to say . . . to your son? Rapist?"

Blaze flicked her gaze to the Sioux woman and knew she understood everything. She held out her free hand and the woman took it.

Warmth flowed up her arm and into her frozen chest. She breathed again. "Bane . . ."

"Look at her," Bane commanded again. "See the mark of the lightning. It has come to strike you."

This time when Bane twisted Jake's neck, Blaze

thought he had killed him, but he was only stunned. With immense effort, Bane swung him up onto his horse. Using his own rope, he bound his prisoner to the saddle.

"Take him into town, Blaze. Deliver him to the sheriff."

Blaze shook her head. "Not without—"

"Go. I will take this woman back to her people. She is injured."

Obediently, Blaze mounted her gelding, then raised her pistol and pointed it at Jake's head. She thumbed the hammer.

"No, Blaze, no. The man who murdered your family, took my mother's soul, and created his own fate will hang. Justice is in the rope, not the swift-flying bullet."

He was right. She knew he was right. Even now she could see the extent and depth of the scarred man's fear. He, too, knew. The storm had finally found him. She reached down and grabbed his horse's reins.

Thunder roared, and lightning streaked the sky. Raindrops fell so hard they bounced upward from the desert floor. Bane came to Lonesome's side. He placed a hand on her thigh.

"It is well done. And it is almost over. Winter comes. Spring follows."

A hot lump rose in her throat. There was so much

to say and no way to say it. Scalding tears were thank-
fully disguised by the rain. Blaze put her heels to her
horse's sides and they were on their way.

CHAPTER
THIRTY-THREE

THE RAIN SLACKED AND FINALLY CEASED. BREAKing through the clouds, the emerging sun felt good on Blaze's cold, damp shoulders. Her mood, however, remained dark and chill. Even the steady, familiar sound of hooves hitting the ground held no comfort for her. Though distance to the town lessened, the distance from Bane increased. Blaze shivered.

And then it happened.

The ground was flat in the direction she rode; flat and featureless. Only an occasional scraggly bush or lonely cactus sprang from the dry, stony ground. She had no warning of the arroyo ahead. There was only time enough to feel Lonesome's muscles bunch before they were flying over the deep, rain-eroded trough in the earth. Then she felt the tension on the reins tightly gripped in her fist.

Jake's horse, underfed and overridden, hadn't the same strength and power as the Appaloosa. His leap was late, weak, and the sudden tension in the reins jarred the bit in his mouth, throwing him off balance. His front feet scrabbled on the opposite wall of the arroyo, but could not gain purchase.

Blaze turned in her saddle to see the panicked animal trying to gain a foothold to climb out of the arroyo. All at once his back feet gained traction, and he lunged upward. She heard Jake grunting as he was jostled about, then scream when his mount, now climbing nearly straight upward overbalanced and fell backward. The reins were pulled roughly from her grip.

The sound was horrible. Jake's scream was abruptly terminated when his horse landed on its back, crushing him. The animal's frightened squeal did not quite cover the sharp crack of bone breaking. Blaze leapt from the saddle, wondering if it had been Jake's skull, spine, or neck.

It didn't matter. He was dead. He had to be.

Jake's horse regained its feet and shook. The man's body, where it was not tightly bound to the saddle, flopped obscenely. Trickles of blood ran from his nostrils. Blaze did not have to feel for the pulse in his neck.

Blaze remounted and looked skyward, surprised to see the sun still shining. It seemed a black cloud had just passed overhead. She felt chilled to the bone.

Bane. She needed to let Bane know what had happened. The blackness of foreboding was overwhelming and would not allow her to move forward. She had to go back.

Slipping and sliding, Lonesome obediently went down the embankment and stood quietly beside the dead man's thin, bay gelding, allowing his rider to easily retrieve the animal's trailing reins.

Blaze tugged gently on the leathers and pressed her heels to her mount's sides. Lonesome started up the opposite embankment, but pressure on the reins nearly jerked her from the saddle. She turned her horse back and dismounted.

Running her hands over the bay gelding's legs revealed only minor cuts and scratches. She pulled on the reins to turn him around, and he moved without hesitation. She led him to the arroyo's steeply sloped side and started upward, stroking his neck and encouraging him all the way. Painfully, grunting and flaring his nostrils, the horse made it to the top.

At a signal, Lonesome returned to Blaze's side and she climbed back into the saddle. When she started off, the gelding followed, although his limp was pronounced. There would be no going back to Bane. It was too far. The animal wouldn't make it. He had endured enough as it was.

At least they were on the town side of the arroyo.

Once again, Blaze started off.

The sheriff slapped at a fly on the back of his neck, dismayed to note the fat roll right above his collar seemed to have grown. He was already in a glum mood when he looked up, and when he saw who had entered his office, his dark mood intensified.

"What'chou want?" he growled.

Blaze stiffened her spine, angry she felt she had to do it. The sheriff was an overgrown worm. "I brought in a body," she replied evenly.

"A *body?*"

"You heard me."

"An' what'chou want me t'do with a body? You lookin' for another bounty? You better show me the Wanted poster if'n you do."

"There's no paper on him. But he's raped and murdered. And worse."

"Says you."

The black premonition clenched hold of her stomach. She had to will her hands not to curl into fists.

The sheriff couldn't control the sneer that twisted his lips. Or the idea that lifted his heart and lightened his mood. "Like I said. Where's the paper?"

"And like *I* said, there isn't any. You didn't require

paper when we brought in the last crew of murderers."

"They were well known 'round these parts. Who's the poor devil whose body you claim you got?"

It was all Blaze could do to keep from reaching for her gun. Hate was like bitter bile in the back of her throat. "I already told you that, too."

"What proof you got he done what you say?"

"My word."

The sheriff choked and sputtered as he rose from his desk. Blaze had to steel herself against cringing. She knew she'd said the wrong thing the instant the words were out of her mouth.

"You just like 'em dead, don'cha, girlie? What happened t'this one? You put a bullet in him?"

"A bullet was too good for him. I was bringing him to stand trial."

"On what evidence?"

How had their plan gone so horribly wrong? It felt like a hand had closed over her heart and squeezed. She took a deep breath and let it out slowly. Barely aware of it, her fingers went to the streak of white in her hair.

"I was a child when he, and others like him, came to my village. They . . ." The hand moved from her heart to her throat. In her mind's eye she saw fallen mothers cradling their lifeless children; Tomas dangling from the end of Jake's rope. And the amused smile on the sheriff's fat face.

The same feeling that had flowed through her limbs when she started digging the mass grave coursed through her again.

She had buried her people; honored them; shed her clothes and her childhood and walked into the mountains. Naked. Where she had been reborn.

Her rebirth was the death of the murderer; the rapist; the maker of Bane and the killer of his mother. The circle was complete. She had completed it.

"They murdered everyone," she finally continued. "Mothers. Old men. Babies. Jake, the dead man, shot me and left me for dead." Once again her fingers lifted to the lightning slash in her hair. She cared nothing about the sneer on the fat man's face.

But he cared about the expression on hers. Arrogant bitch, thinking she could kill a man and bald-faced lie to him about it. He stood up and slammed his palms on his desk. The holstered pistol almost seemed to jump into his hand.

"How'd he die?" the sheriff demanded.

Blaze kept her eye on the gun. Was he going to try to shoot her? The muscles in her legs tensed and her fingers flexed.

"His horse flipped over. Crushed him."

"*That* sounds familiar. Herd o' buffalo . . . horse . . ."

The sheriff's guffaw took Blaze completely by surprise.

CHAPTER
THIRTY-FOUR

RING RODE UP TO CARRIE'S FRONT PORCH, THEN PAST
it. No need to rush right in with bad news. No, not
bad news. Devastating news. Swallowing something
rising unpleasantly in the back of his throat, Ring dismounted and led his horse to one of the corrals. He
took his time removing the tack and letting the animal
loose in the paddock.

The mare immediately buckled her legs and sank
into the dust for a good roll. Ring paused a moment
more to watch her. With dragging steps he finally
turned and walked back to the neat and modest house
he had come to call home.

Carrie reached out and took one of Bane's hands
when she heard the familiar footsteps on the front
porch. "More coffee?"

Bane didn't bother to answer. He couldn't. His

tongue was frozen to the roof of his mouth. He watched Ring saunter through the door.

Though things had begun badly between them, the men had become friends. Such good friends, in fact, Bane didn't need to hear the words. He saw the message in Ring's expression.

"Bane."

Bane rose, careful not to knock over his chair, and took Ring's outstretched hand. The pressure of Ring's grip was not comforting, but Bane drew a measure of strength from the reason for it. When Ring relaxed his grip, Bane dropped his hands to his sides and waited for the words that would drive the knife into his heart.

"They . . . they put her on trial, Bane."

"Oh, no!" Carrie's hands covered her mouth.

Ring gave her an almost-imperceptible nod, and she forced her hands into her lap.

"When?"

Ring swallowed, Adam's apple bobbing. He stroked a thumb along the edge of his jaw and tried to still the mad beating of his heart.

"It's . . . it's over, Bane."

What seemed like a long, long time ago he had stood on a mountaintop with the woman who had become his mate and said, "There is no heaven for people like us. Only hell."

He had not fully realized the truth or scope of his

prophetic words until this moment.

"And . . . ?"

Bane could not finish the question, just as he knew Ring could not offer a response without prompting. He saw the tears in his friend's eyes and knew he would see them on Carrie's cheeks as well. He did not look at her when she again took his hand. Every fiber of his being was focused on remaining calm and strong. For Blaze.

Ring really didn't know if he could say the words or not. He didn't know if he had the strength to restrain Bane. But, in the end, he knew he could not remain silent.

"She . . . they . . ." Ring looked away and cleared his throat. With the greatest effort of will he had ever exercised, he turned back to Bane.

"They condemned her to hang."

Carrie started to sob. She couldn't help it. Nor could she prevent the agonized "Noooo," which was wrung from the core of her soul. As long as she lived, she would never know how Bane restrained himself from running from the house, getting on a horse, and rushing to Blaze's side. Disbelieving, lower lip caught in her teeth, tears pouring down her cheeks, she watched him stand straight and tall and silent.

Until the veins in his neck suddenly corded, and he slammed a fist into the palm of his other hand.

"Bane." Ring grabbed his friend's wrists. "We'll do something. Sit down. Let's talk."

Bane shook his head as if in denial. "She can't hang. She can't. I promised her. I promised."

The day her parents were murdered Carrie thought she had experienced the most emotional moment in her life. She'd been wrong.

Bane forced himself to think of lifting his rifle and taking aim. He stilled both mind and body. Recalling the facts he had earlier garnered from Ring, he said, "There was no paper on the gang we brought in. Why—"

"You know," Ring replied heavily. "Don't make me have to say the words."

No. Ring was correct. He would not speak the lie aloud. To speak it would only spread the venom and sickness of it.

Never in his life had Bane felt, or given in to, a feeling of weakness. But never in his life had he been delivered such a blow. Pulling back the chair he had vacated, he sank into the seat. Ring sat across the table from him and reached out a hand. Bane took it.

Ring briefly dropped his chin to his chest. Looking Bane in the eye again was the hardest thing he'd ever had to do.

"Bane, I . . . I have a date. But I also have a plan."

There was nothing he could do. Not yet. Ring's plan was a good one. Dangerous. Difficult. But their only hope.

Nevertheless, he was unbearably restless. When he finally heard the regular sounds of deep breathing coming from the loft, Bane grabbed his bedroll and left the house.

He didn't go far. The moon and stars were obscured by clouds, and he was on foot. When he knew it wasn't safe to go farther, he dropped his bedroll, spread it out and lay down.

At least he was closer to her. He closed his eyes and breathed in the scent of her on the wind.

CHAPTER THIRTY-FIVE

HE HAD LEARNED TO HANDLE A KNIFE AS A VERY young boy. Growing older it became a part of him. Guns had come later, but he was no less skillful in their use. So why, now, did he doubt his ability?

Bane knew, as surely as he knew his next breath would come whether he willed it or not. But he could not give the thought voice in his heart. He must risk nothing that might weaken him.

The sun beat on his head and shoulders but the air was cold. A chill wind whipped a length of long, black hair in his eyes. Irritated, he pushed it behind an ear, but the breeze promptly loosed it again.

Slowly, carefully, Bane set the rifle on its stock and leaned it against the side of the building where he stood vigil, then retied the rawhide strip around his gathered hair. He fingered the hilt of his knife, palmed it, and picked up the rifle.

His post was three buildings down from the gallows. He sighted on the noose. Felt the weight of the knife in his hand.

She must not hang. She would not. He had promised. One way or another, he would deliver her from the noose.

The babble of voices reached Bane. Had they taken her from the jail? For the merest fraction of a second, he raised his gaze from the rope to the rooftop of another building on the far side of the gallows from him.

Carrie's hair, like his, lifted in the wind. He saw the soft, red-blond color of it and fastened his eyes back on the rope. He wondered if she, too, heard the voices and understood the meaning of them.

When Bane was young, he had known the love of his mother and the people of his village. When he became a man, only the passion of revenge lived in his heart. He had been alone until he met one other who walked the same lonely road. She had awakened something in him he had not known remained alive. It would die forever if he failed in his mission.

The fear of the death of his heart must not weaken him. In weakness he would fail. He banned the surge of debilitating warmth that flowed though his belly and tried to reach his arms and legs when he saw her at last. But he found he could not draw a deep breath until he saw Carrie raise her arm in signal to Ring.

He increased his pressure on the trigger when she approached the steps to the gallows, the fat sheriff right behind her. And then the sound he heard was not the murmur of voices, but the thunder of hooves. The sheriff shook his head as if to clear away a sound he thought he really shouldn't be hearing, slipped the hood over his prisoner's head, and settled the noose around her neck. Tightened it. Gave the signal to open the trapdoor . . .

Bane had to will himself not to look when the herd of horses pounded into town.

The townspeople scattered, screaming.

The trapdoor opened.

Bane fired.

Though he never planned for failure, he did plan for success. The knife was on its way to the target even as he started running.

It was not the sheriff's happiest day. He didn't like the woman, but hanging her didn't give him the pleasure he thought it would. And it was going to make him infamous. He hadn't realized, until it was too late, how far her fame had spread. Her and her half-breed sidekick. So he merely grunted and turned away when the man appeared, as if out of nowhere, and cut down the body.

Although it seemed someone had beat him to it. Vaguely puzzled, the sheriff scratched his head as he looked down through the open trapdoor and watched the Indian scoop the dead woman off the ground and into his arms.

Then he turned to his next problem. Where in hell had all those damn horses come from, and what were they doing running wild through the town?

Had he been swift enough? His aim had been true, but had it been in time? Had he broken his promise?

Dodging the milling horses, Blaze cradled in his arms, Bane searched for Ring and Carrie. But it was Ring who first spotted Bane, and his gut twisted sickeningly when he saw Blaze's apparently lifeless form. Had their elaborate plan all been for naught? When Ring saw the tears streaming down Bane's face, he knew they had lost the race.

EPILOGUE

BANE WAS SURPRISED BY THE NUMBER OF PEOPLE WHO attended the funeral. According to Ring, their names had become legend. The lightning and the thunder, bounty hunters. Sympathy for Bane, by himself, had swelled the ranks of the mourners. His ride out of town after the hanging, with Blaze in his arms, had not gone unnoticed.

It hadn't taken Ring long to bang together a coffin. They had brought it into town, to the cemetery, in the back of a wagon. By the time they reached the grave-yard gate, there was a long line of people behind them.

Though Bane had not asked him, the local minis-ter had taken pity on him and said a few words at the graveside. When he was done, he simply walked away, many of the mourners trailing behind him. Only Bane, Ring, and Carrie remained with the coffin as the cemetery's caretaker halfheartedly shoveled dirt into the grave. The sheriff stood off to one side, hands shoved in his pockets. When Bane glanced in his direction, he had the grace to look chagrined.

Answering Ring's question, Bane raised his voice to make sure the sheriff overheard. With soul-deep satisfaction, Bane noticed the chagrined expression change to one of sympathy. When he concluded his story, Carrie, with tears in her eyes, put a gentle hand on his forearm. Ring tipped his hat back and wiped a tear from his own eye.

"Thanks for the tellin', Bane," he said at length. "I'm just so sorry she never got the chance to tell me that story herself."

Bane walked a few steps away from the grave, then turned back to Ring and Carrie. "And now the story of her life is over, too."

The sheriff finally backed away, hat pulled down low over his eyes. Bane left the cemetery and mounted his black mare. Carrie caught up with him before he could ride away, however, and laid a hand on his leg.

"Where are you going, Bane?" she asked softly. "What are you going to do now?"

Bane remained still and silent while he watched the sheriff walk away from them.

"You can always stay with us, you know," Carrie added. "In fact, I wish you would. Take some time.

Think on what you're going to do next. We'd be proud to have you."

In response, Bane began backing his horse. Carrie's hand slipped from his knee.

"She didn't hang," Ring said suddenly, filling the uncomfortable silence. "At least she didn't die hangin'. You did your best by her. You kept your promise, Bane. She didn't die from hangin'."

Bane nodded once, briefly, and put his heels to the black mare's sides. Ring and Carrie watched him, standing side by side and holding hands, until the only thing they could see was a vanishing trail of dust. Then they mounted their own horses and rode off in the opposite direction.

The sun was setting, and the already-chill air was getting downright cold when Ring and Carrie pulled into the camp. Bane had a fire going, and they dismounted quickly to stand near its warmth.

"No one trailed us, Bane. Don't worry," Ring said, rubbing his hands together briskly. "You're safe. Both of ya, so long's you never ride this way again. The sheriff, the whole town bought it."

Bane moved closer to Blaze and put a protective arm around her shoulder. With his free hand, he lightly touched the raw, red marks on her neck.

"That was a mighty close call," Ring said, and let out a long, slow breath of delayed relief.

Blaze lifted a hand to cover Bane's fingers at her throat. His was a touch she had thought she would never feel again, and it was incredibly precious to her. And although she was reluctant to leave his side—ever again—an overwhelming rush of love compelled her.

It seemed to Carrie she had been doing nothing for days except crying. It had started when she learned of Blaze's fate and hadn't stopped until she realized Blaze really was alive. Bane's blade had severed the rope in the nick of time.

The tears had flowed again at the "funeral" when she, along with Ring, heard Bane tell Blaze's story from the beginning. And now she cried once more as she hugged the brave and amazing young woman she had come to call a friend.

Would their paths ever cross again, she wondered? In the same moment she doubted it. As Ring had said, they would never be able to come this way again and risk the sheriff finding out Blaze wasn't in that grave after all—only a weighted coffin. Stifling a sob, she hugged Blaze tighter. Only when she felt Ring's comforting arm around her shoulders did she reluctantly release her friend.

There were no words to tell Ring what was in her

heart, so Blaze simply hugged him as she had Carrie. Besides, the lump in her throat was powerfully painful, and she probably couldn't have spoken if she *had* managed to find adequate words.

Ring looked equally at a loss. When Blaze finally eased away from him, however, he held out a hand and touched the streak in her hair.

"Blaze," he murmured. "It was a good name."

Her tears overflowed at last. Blaze pressed a hand over her heart and turned back to Bane. He had already saddled their horses, and she silently thanked him for his understanding.

She did not look back even once as they rode away.

The storm was over.

A new, bright day had dawned.

Neither of them would ever have to look back again.